ANXIETY IN THE WILDERNESS

SHORT STORIES

KATHLEEN PATRICK

For Bob Terhaar, the love of my life.

NOTE FROM THE AUTHOR

These stories were written over several years, and the settings span several decades. They do not need to be read in any order, although I like to think there is a certain symmetry in doing so. Some of the characters exist only in these pages; others moved on to bigger stories. Perhaps you'll meet up with them again.

MY NEIGHBOR STILL MOWS THE LAWN

Because there is no bringing her back.
The grass grows, continues growing and
There is nothing else to be done.
We all mow our lawns,
Think about the hole left where
Love used to be and put
One foot in front of the other,
Pushing the mower in the Sunday morning heat.
I look out my window at the trees changing
Color and want to comfort a brother
Miles away with no grass to mow.
He finds other things to push.
He does not recognize his life,
Says he watches his days as if
He were an interloper dancing the dance
Of an imposter, each foot carefully placed.
The world seems filled
With the moan of mowers.
The sound fills the air with sadness.
It echoes against my heart.

CONTENTS

1

LETTERS HOME

I wanted noise. There was a cafe about seven blocks from my mother's home, and Saturday night at nine-thirty was a good time to look for people talking over coffee, talking loudly for the sake of a story above the clanking dishes and the corner jukebox.

The old cafe resembled a hunting lodge with polished pine and dusty, stuffed trophies adorning the walls. I sat in one of the booths, its table's shellacked-wood surface gouged and eloquent with age. The coffee was good, and there was plenty of noise.

"You get that turned over by midweek, and I'll be glad to take the Deere off your hands. I still got a quarter up near Nelson's that I haven't touched yet. The fields are ready, I tell ya." A farmer lifted his feed cap, scratching his head for proper emphasis. His friend nodded, dipping the corner of a sweet roll into his coffee.

"You can count on it. I better be out of that section before Wednesday, or all hell is gonna break loose. You heard the weather?" He raised his finger, motioning to the waitress for more coffee.

I was used to silence. But sometimes, especially now when I was back home visiting my mother, I craved the city noises, the sounds of neighbors through thin walls, a car trying to bring its cold bones back to life, a wavering siren. There never was enough sound in our home.

MY MOTHER NEVER WASTED WORDS. She was the kind who sent birthday cards and just signed them "Mom." Even when I hadn't heard from her for months, that was it — "Mom" —no news and no lost words. Once I forgot my checkbook on the kitchen table when I left after the Christmas holidays. Four days later, it arrived in the mail with a small note saying, "Seems this was it. Mom." I translated that into "I don't think you left anything else, at least that I found. If you did, I will mail it later." I also liked to think it meant "So enjoyed having you home for Christmas. Do come again soon. I love you. Mom." I often indulged in such childish fortunetelling concerning what my mother was feeling and not saying. It was the way I had grown up.

When I was stretching out of my teens and watching friends get drafted, it was as if life began to happen in slow motion. The fast pace of childhood was gone. Mother seemed to grow even further into herself, as if the quakes from the bombs in Vietnam could reach as far as Iowa and hurt her in some new way. Jerry and I kept conversation in the house, kept the supper table alive with voices, even if we were usually arguing. He was my older brother, and the fighting was rarely in earnest. But after he left, it was Mother and me and "Pass the cream, please" and "No, thank you, I've had enough." I found myself alone in the house with her, and at supper the sound of the clock in the dining room overwhelmed me.

JERRY WAS twenty when he enlisted. Filled with Uncle Sam ideas about the war, he wanted to get involved. He had been captain of his football team, and some of that "huddle instinct" seemed to transfer into his life after graduation. He didn't know what to do with it. The action didn't seem to be in a business degree at the University of Iowa. I was a senior in high school and didn't have much of an opinion about it one way or the other until Jerry was in Vietnam. Then I read the papers and tried to make sense of the war.

Jerry used to give me rides places after he got his license, and I was still too young to drive. We talked then, as soon as we left the house. He started calling me "kid" and playing gangster like he was kidnapping me or something, but we talked. He asked me if I had enough money and if the man of my dreams would be at the game. I rolled down my window even in early March when the cold brought tears to my eyes. I held out my hand, flat-palmed, riding the currents and talking his arm off. That's what he used to say: "Okay, kid, here's your stop. Now quit talking my arm off and get out. I'll pick you up at ten. You read time, kid? Ten o'clock." And then he smiled all white teeth and light freckles. I missed Jerry when he was gone.

As usual, Mother absorbed things silently. My father died when I was six years old. Mother was alone with two grade school children, a house, and no job. She never cried. Relatives were at our house for three or four days for the funeral, and she didn't shed one tear the entire time. Finally, one afternoon, when the last of the friends had gone, I was standing near the living-room window watching the rain and tracing trees in the moisture on the pane. I heard her in her bedroom weeping softly, but I never saw a single tear.

BEFORE JERRY LEFT for his tour of duty, he came back to Iowa on a ten-day leave. Mother had cleaned his room and moved the television in near his bed. Jerry used to sneak the TV up to his room at night to watch the late movies. Mother had never approved. "If you want to watch the program that badly, sit on the couch and watch it with the rest of the family," she said quietly as she sat knitting. Often she did not say another word the entire evening. Moving the television into his room was her way of welcoming him home.

Jerry arrived with short hair and bragged about the things he had learned in basic. "It's more of a workout than spring training ever was, but I'm getting the biceps in shape and improving my speed a lot. You should see this big guy in our unit on the self-defense maneuvers. God, is he incredible! I hope the enemy isn't that big!" He practiced his rifle drills with a broom. Mother seemed to grow nervous as she feigned being impressed.

The day he went back, she gave him a bundle of envelopes. As close to hugging him as she would ever come, she had tied fifty white envelopes in a bundle. Each one was addressed to her in neat, calculated print-ing. Each one was empty and unsealed. She presented the envelopes to him in a slow, tired voice. "I have only one thing to request, as a mother. I hope you see fit to go along with my foolish indulgence. If you would just post one of these a week, simply seal it and add postage, I would know you were okay. I don't expect you to write a letter inside each one of them, of course, but if you would just send it to me, I would feel better." She paused awkwardly and seemed to be working at forming a final sentence. She looked down at her feet and added, "I guess that's all."

In the following year, Mother retrieved her envelopes as if they were carrier pigeons. Some were empty, some read like entries in the high-school yearbook full of promises and funny stories, and others contained chilling words from a young man in the middle of a war. Occasionally the letters arrived late or skipped a week altogether. It was difficult to be on time in a war without logic. But when they did not arrive, Mother stopped eating and forgot to mail out her bills or put gasoline in her car. It was as if she nearly stopped breathing, terrified of what the lapse could mean. Usually, however, they arrived at weekly intervals and were added to the neatly stacked pile on the bureau near her bed.

It was odd, living in a house with the same woman I had lived with all of my life and yet feeling as if no one was ever home. I hadn't realized the important part Jerry played in keeping it all alive for me, even in small ways. I needed to reach out.

MY WAR EFFORT consisted of letters to Jerry twice a week. Mother sent him articles from *Field and Stream* about certain fishing techniques he would want to try when he got home. Sometimes she sent him clippings from the hometown paper with high school sports scores.

Rarely did she write, and when she did, it was usually four or five words added on to some clipping.

JERRY CAME HOME. The three of us painted the house that summer. It was a time for celebrating adulthood. Jerry and I were no longer at the bickering age, and we could enjoy each other's company. Our letters seemed to have drawn us closer as well. We could talk easily for the first time in a house that had seemed silent so long.

"All right, woman, look here. If you plan to do a decent job on this wall, you have to start in the corner. Otherwise I'm going to have to spend the rest of the day covering up your Picasso prints on the ceiling. Do you understand, woman?" Jerry stood with his feet firmly planted, assuming military authority. He had adopted a new saying, "All right, woman," and applied it to me whenever he had a suggestion about how the painting should be done, where we should proceed, what we should be listening to on the radio. He was acknowledging my age; we were friends. In her quiet way, Mother obviously enjoyed having us together again, joking and smiling next to her. The weight had been removed from her chest, a weight that existed because of the possibilities.

· · ·

I was thinking about her slight smile when the door of the cafe opened to a man already laughing, his head slightly back, the rumble of soft laughter filling the room. Dressed in stiff new jeans and a soft corduroy shirt, he swung his coat over the counter stool like a cowboy saddling up.

His causal control interested me. His mustache interested me. Black, cornrowed hair formed straight lines and neat angles across his head, all connected in a smooth pattern like veins on the back of a hand. His strong, sharp cheekbones made him handsome, but his best feature was his full mustache. When he smiled or laughed, which he did frequently, the hair would rise to reveal a dark cave of beautiful teeth.

I ordered another cup of coffee, watching. People seemed to flow over to him, not obeying the rules for distance as I knew them. The waitress, about forty and graying at the temples, placed her hand on his when he said he liked the fresh pie. A thank-you gesture, I thought, a sincere thanks a lot, open and easy. He smiled.

An older man in a suit and overcoat walked up and greeted him with a slap on the back, "How's it going, stranger? You're looking good. How do you like this weather? It's got my bones a little concerned—don't like the moisture, no sir."

"Well, I think it beats the snow, actually, but give me another two or three weeks, and I'll recommend Iowa springtime to anyone. Did you hear about Howard last night?"

It was difficult to hear everything, but I was not ashamed of my eavesdropping. As I said, on this visit home I wanted noise. I listened. He seemed able to converse with everyone. He gave a young woman a recipe for cooking pheasant so that the wild taste was most appealing. I watched a smile wash over the waitress's face when he remarked, "The new tables in the back look about as nice as that new hairdo on you, Sarah. I must say, very attractive."

I wanted to ask him why it was so easy for him, why he talked so much, why I could not seem to get the hang of it myself. Bitterness was growing inside me, and it did not sit well with my sorrow. I wanted to draw some conclusions before going back home. I wanted to understand my mother's scarce words, so that I could gather a few of my own before morning.

That evening at supper, I commented on the changes she was making in the house. Mother was never one for extreme neatness. She had always like piles, neat orderly piles, but things out in the open nonetheless. Monthly bills were usually stacked on the table near the telephone. Mail order catalogues were piled to serve as a doorstop. Newspapers lay beside the sofa in the living room, but now the piles were gone. All the table tops were clean and gleaming with furniture polish.

My old bedroom was filling with cardboard boxes, boxes that contained birth certificates, wedding announcements, Jerry's letters, and my high school yearbooks. Old dishes were wrapped and stacked like a display for a rummage sale. After finishing supper and drinking a cup of coffee, I casually asked, "Mother, are you planning on having a sale? Or remodeling? I noticed all the boxes in my old room."

She quickly stood, went to the stove, and returned with the coffeepot. "Would you like more coffee?"

I was used to her curt way of smoothing out questions into nothingness, so that life would flow along quickly and on track. I said I would and held out my cup.

After we washed the supper dishes, she delivered one of her infrequent speeches. Like her request when Jerry was leaving for his plane, it sounded so final that I did not say a word. I was reading in the living room when she walked in holding her navy winter coat in a dry-cleaning bag. She looked preoccupied but not exceptionally worried. It was like she was checking things off from a list she needed to complete during my visit. She sat on the edge of the sofa, her small frame illuminated by the reading lamp.

She began with measured words in her soft voice. "There are some things you should know. I suspect you are the one to tell, as Jerry lives so far away and never was very good about such things. Don't ask any questions just now…in the morning perhaps…but think about it a bit tonight. I think that is more rational, the best way to go about things. I am going to be gone soon. I've put things in order, taken care to organize and label every-thing. I think the house should be sold. Of course, you and Jerry have a good deal to say about that; you both spent much of your lives here. You may do as you wish." She smoothed the plastic over her winter coat with small, measured strokes. Then, as if in the room alone, she began picking lint off the arm of the sofa. I didn't speak. I watched her hands moving and waited for her to continue.

Finally, she sighed deeply and said, "I'm writing things down as I think of them. I think it will help. I'll want to finalize some things with you, but I am tired, and I think the morning is the best time. I'm going to bed. The television doesn't bother me if you wish to watch it later. Good night."

With that, she touched my arm with her warm, light hand. I looked at that hand, the veins suddenly a darker blue and nearer the surface, the wrinkles deep and aged, the hand of a frail old woman. She left slowly, her back bent slightly forward and curving into herself. She took small steps. I had never considered the idea that my mother was growing old. Now she spoke of selling the house, leaving business matters to her children. I needed fresh air.

. . .

SITTING in the cafe after three cups of coffee, I was confused, and yet I felt a familiar pain. My mother was mailing empty envelopes to me, not telling me anything but saying that everything would be all right. Her careful, calculated handwriting spelled out "Well, it seems this is it." She was dying and doing it her way.

I wanted some direction, some instruction as to how I should handle myself at our little conference in the morning. Unaccustomed to dealing with my feelings openly, I felt anger and self-pity. I wanted to cry, to express something to the mother I had never seen cry. I wanted to be consoled.

The man with the mustache was putting on his coat, getting ready to leave. I contemplated leaving at the same time, brushing against his arm as I went by as a good-luck charm. I wanted to be close to someone just then, but he reached the door, turned, smiled, and was gone.

He took his warmth with him like a wool sweater. I saw no further reason to stay out in the night looking for noise, but after walking the cracked sidewalk back to my mother's house, I was unable to go inside. The porch smelled of early lilacs. I wanted to read my mother's palm, to discover what she was not going to tell me in the morning when I would remain as stiff and formal as she wished while she completed the checklist and bound the package of ghost-white envelopes with a new ribbon. I wanted to go beyond, but I had not learned how.

I knew I would take the envelopes in silence. I knew some would be empty, some would be filled with promises and pastel memories, and others would contain honest, frightened notes, employing very few words.

2

METEOR SHOWERS

The greatest night to wish on falling stars since the Civil War, and I sit here under the thick Minnesota clouds and stare at the TV. There's no sound, since the last electrical storm blew it out. One good bolt of lightning over the lake, and Katherine Hepburn looked at Spencer Tracy, and I don't know what the hell she said.

Storms out in the country can be rather comforting. I like listening to the rain as it hits the side of the house and taps against the glass as if I have company. It cools off then, and I can open up the windows and sleep in the fresh breeze.

It's been a hot, humid summer. Lots of rain. The corn looks like fairytale beanstalks when I go walking at night. I like to walk between the rows. I learned never to step across rows; my sense of direction is bad, and one night I ended up wandering around in that damn field till almost ten-thirty, and the mosquitoes had eaten me alive.

Now, I walk all the way down one row and then back up another. It's a quarter section and a good walk. Anyway, the corn is way over my head, and I can smell the sweet greenness as it all ripens and stretches toward the sky.

The night I got lost, I started watching the stars, thinking maybe the Big Dipper would lead me, you know, the North Star off the end of the bowl and all that. But I didn't know if my house was north or east or whatever from where I was, so I just watched the stars and followed a row to its end.

I ended up over by the Oliver's place. They have twin boys in my health class. They study hard and read what they are assigned, but they always wear the same shirts, so they look identical, and it kind of gives me the creeps. Like maybe they could get lost in each other.

They seem to enjoy tricking people, never really letting on who's who. I guess last year before I was here, they dressed different and had different haircuts, and no one had any trouble telling them apart. Jeff was a little quieter and read a lot. Josh was the joker and the leader, but then this summer Mr. Oliver shot himself in the haymow at their second farm, and the boys fused into a matched set. Since I'm their health teacher, I talked to them to see if they'd had any counseling or anything, as if

I'm one to talk, but they just looked at me like I was from another planet. I took it as a no.

The meteor shower is the result of some big litterbug comet crossing the earth's path. The meteors are supposed to be falling from one to twelve a minute. Now that's real wishing material. Of course, we end up with a thick, clouded sky and no breeze. I went out earlier to see if maybe there was a hole through the clouds, a window or something where there was a chance, but it's a tent of black. No light. No falling stars.

The loons are making a lot of noise. I'm renting this house for the school year. I have to be out in June because the woman who owns the land wants to try renting it out to fishermen next summer, one week at a time. I guess the lake is full of bass. I haven't decided where I'll go next summer. I suppose it depends if I get another contract. I'm not sure I will. Whenever you teach things like birth control and how to avoid AIDS, you don't get real popular with the conservative folks in town. Not that I'd be popular with them anyway, but I got the curriculum approved by the school board, so we'll see.

I guess last year Jeff was the "A" student and Josh usually got B's and C's. This year they both pull straight A's, and sometimes teachers speculate in the lounge about which kid was actually in their room taking the test third hour. The sad and lost identical-twin conspiracy.

. . .

I FEEL SORRY FOR THEM. So many farm families are trying to figure out how to make it. Maybe Mr. Oliver saw his boys getting older and knew at least one of them wanted to go to college, and he wasn't getting a good price for anything he grew anymore, and his dairy production wasn't big enough or sophisticated enough to compete. Maybe he saw the writing on the wall, saw the dwindling bank account. Maybe his wife said she didn't think she loved him, didn't think she'd ever loved him. Maybe she said she loved him so much she didn't know how she could ever live without him. Maybe he was dying before he killed himself.

No real gossip around town about that. In a small farming community when a farmer ends his life, everyone just shakes their heads, wipes their eyes, goes to the funeral, and hopes like hell it doesn't touch anyone even closer to them next time.

My family didn't farm. Dad ran a small shoe store in a small town, and sometimes we had some pretty good years. I know about farming because my last two jobs were in farming communities too. The breadbasket in crisis. I left my first job because I could coach varsity volleyball at the next one. My main sport. Better pay. But then, after only one year, they started making cutbacks, and I was the first to go. We won districts and had a real chance at regions if Glenda Herbert hadn't injured that right knee.

So, then I started over again. Unpacking boxes, walking in corn fields, getting ready for another year of not knowing a soul. I moved in at the beginning of July. I had to be out of my old place in Crookston, and I'd already signed a contract and found this great deal in the local paper for an old farm house out on Tyler Lake.

Right away, when I moved in, I felt a little odd about this place. Odd but comfortable. I didn't get a phone since I didn't know anyone to call anyway, and no one was going to be calling me. It was clearly over when I left Crookston. Over and done with. Thanks but don't call me, I'll call you. You know. So I didn't get a phone. Like I had the last word. The deposit was too damn much anyway, until I started getting a check again.

It was something about the house; I didn't feel lonely. It was just me and occasionally the sound of the loons down in the weedy shallows of the lake. I ran around the section every morning and spent most of the day hanging around the house planning my classes for the fall, reading the new textbook I'd be using.

I didn't start hearing noises until I'd been there almost a month. Then it was like the old house was coming to life. Windows slid down at night. A common thing with old sashes and pulls, I thought. Doors slammed. No big deal. But one morning, when I woke up and went down to the kitchen, there was a glass of orange juice sitting on the kitchen table like it was waiting for me. I didn't pour it. I checked my front door and it was locked. No window screens broken. It was pretty damn weird. Then about a week later, I found my tennis racket in the middle of the living room floor with a tennis ball laying right on the strings. I keep my tennis racket in a case by the back door.

I started to get pretty upset with that one. I started imagining that someone was watching me, playing tricks on me, trying to let me know that they too had snooped in my private life and knew all the secrets hidden there. I tell you, it felt very unsettling, and yet part of me was calm and relaxed about the whole thing.

The Thursday before school started, I went over to pay my landlady, a nice old woman named Hilda, and told her I was worried someone was getting into the house. She stood at the doorway in a flowered house-dress. She was a short, plump woman with beautiful gray hair.

"What do you mean 'getting in' dear?" she asked.

"I mean, coming into my house and moving stuff around. My stuff."

Hilda paused a moment and then opened the screen door wider. "You'd better come in for a cup of tea, dear. Sounds to me like we need to talk."

She sat me down at her kitchen table and served me warm chocolate chip cookies and tea like I was the neighborhood kid over to pay a visit. I felt welcomed and content, and then she started to tell me about the ghost. Well, she thought maybe there was a ghost at the old place, but it was nothing to be concerned about. All these years it's never been unfriendly, just a bit mischievous and curious, she said.

Nothing much shocks me anymore, so I took a sip of my tea but it was still too hot, and I burned my tongue. She got out some cream to cool it off, poured it for me, picked up my spoon, and stirred it.

"I would have told you, if I'd thought she was going to act up. I'd have given you the opportunity not to take the place if you wanted, and of course you can still leave, but it is usually very quiet. She doesn't get very active around most people. You must be a sensitive, open soul. She must like you."

"Excuse me?" I said.

"She was always around when I lived at the old house. I lived there twenty years. Oh," Hilda noticed my confused look. "Well, I think it is a she. They say spirits are usually people who have died in the house and aren't ready for the next world yet, so I did some checking, lord, years ago now. A young woman died giving birth in that house. I believe it was back in 1932 or '33. I always figured she just wanted some company. Never caused me any trouble."

I sat there not able to think of anything to say. Was the old woman a nut?

"Does it bother you?" Hilda asked. "Do you want out of your lease?"

"No. I don't think so." I knew I'd never find a place as big and nice as this one for the price.

"At night, just leave a light on over the sink in the kitchen. It seems to keep things calmed down. Let me know if anything really odd happens."

I told her about the orange juice and the tennis racket. She chuckled and told me about the folded laundry and the apple pie. I thanked her and went home. To my ghost. Casper and I, sharing a house. A new roommate. Another woman to confuse and mess up my life.

ANYWAY, a few weeks went by, school started, the corn began to yellow and dry up, and I left the kitchen light on at night. Things quieted down.

I already told you about Mr. Oliver. My neighbor, across one massive corn field. My students' father. Gone. I wonder if he has left the farm yet. I mean, if you buy into any of this spirit stuff. Or maybe the boys are the ghosts, apparitions taking the place of two normal, happy farm kids with morning chores and lives ahead of them. Two kids who now run the place and try to get everything done in the midst of trying to be teenagers. Two identical faces trying to make a mother smile, trying to put things back in place when so many of the pieces are missing.

I've taken to talking to my housemate. I wonder how a pregnant body would feel. I wonder how dying so young in the middle of giving birth would feel. Did she see her child? Was it a boy or a girl? Did it have a name? And I wonder about the child. Did she grow up missing her mother? Wondering what it meant to be a female? Wondering how she would turn out, if she would ever be a mother, if she would ever fit in.

I think about stacks of shoe boxes full of new leather shoes at my dad's store, about standing between two rows of shelves that reach over my head, and about peeking through at little girls from my school trying on new shoes. Girls with blonde curls and lace-trimmed socks. And later, working in the store, helping high school girls in hose find sophisticated pumps to wear to the prom.

I go outside again to check the cloud cover with the hope that there might be a small patch of clear sky. A window for wishing. But the sky is black, and the night is getting late.

Back inside, I turn off the TV and close the shades. I turn on the light in the kitchen and go up to bed. It isn't so bad living with a ghost. I try to make us as comfortable as possible, and these days, that is not an easy thing to do.

3

ANXIETY IN THE WILDERNESS

R eagan Mueller sat in her champagne-colored Infiniti in the middle lane of the freeway, going nowhere. She was headed downtown. It was 7:46 a.m., and traffic was at a dead halt.

She turned up the music, adjusted the air, and closed her eyes. Tracy Chapman crooned "Stand by Me." Reagan thought about William. He'd gotten home late last night after she'd gone to bed and was gone this morning before she woke up. She didn't enjoy his life going on around her like some kind of movie she was only allowed to watch. It made her nervous and a little sad; something important was missing. She thought about the bear for the first time that morning.

Reagan tried to think of other things. The Hadley deposition was scheduled for eleven. She needed to review the transcripts and get a letter off to BCW Sales before that. Hopefully, her secretary had finished typing the draft of the Skylar motion.

She thought about the bear more and more all the time. It wasn't a matter of choice, but rather an unpleasant known fact that wouldn't go away, like headlines in the paper, like the six o'clock news, like William working later and later, catching dinner downtown. Reagan spent increasingly more time trying to trick her brain into thinking about something else.

In early June, she and William had vacationed on the Susitna River in Alaska. Paul, William's best friend from high school, had moved up there years ago with his wife, Cassandra. They bought some land, built a cabin, and said good-bye to Wall Street.

The vacation had been planned for two or three years, but something always interfered. One of Reagan's legal cases, some top priority at William's office, a friend's wedding, or her parents' fortieth anniversary. Finally, their suitcases full of flannel shirts, jeans, and sweatshirts, they arrived in the Anchorage airport and left with Paul and Cass in a four-wheel drive Jeep.

Reagan had met Paul and Cassandra at William's tenth class reunion. They went out to dinner, talked about sports and New York theater, complained about the big rat race. Paul was ready to leave it behind. He already had plans and the blueprints for a log cabin. He'd read the books on self-sufficiency. Cass taught art at a New York

Community College. She said she could paint anywhere. She was ready for a change too.

Six years later, the four of them pulled into a gravel parking lot near some railroad tracks about a hundred miles from Anchorage.

"This is it," Paul said. "The neighborhood parking garage."

Cass smiled. She looked like Reagan remembered her: long blonde hair, slim, young looking. Paul had grown a beard and let his sandy-brown hair grow out. There was a little gray. He looked like he belonged in Alaska. Reagan hardly recognized him in the airport.

They got out of the Jeep, and Paul disappeared into the trees surrounding three sides of the square lot. He returned in a few minutes driving a three-wheeler, pulling a small trailer with a bed about three feet by three feet.

"Put your suitcases in here." Paul loaded a couple of boxes of groceries out of the back of the Jeep. "Now comes the fun part."

Cass put her hands in the front pockets of her jeans and smiled apologetically. "I don't know how much Paul told you about our place, but there's no road access, so we need to walk in. You can get there on the river by boat, or in the winter we use snow machines a lot, but this is the only land access." Cass looked at Reagan's puzzled face. "Along the railroad tracks. Come on, it's a pretty walk." She smiled.

Paul started up the three-wheeler, now packed with supplies and suitcases, and headed down a well-worn path to the railroad tracks. The tracks were raised, with rather steep banks on both sides. Paul drove the three-wheeler on the left side at a rather precarious slant.

William laughed, his eyebrows raised. "Seriously?"

"Absolutely. Come on." Cass tightened the lace on her hiking boot and headed up the incline to the flat part of the tracks. Reagan looked down at her soft leather boots and wondered how long they'd last.

Soon all three of them were walking down the tracks, following the buzz of the three-wheeler out ahead of them, walking on the railroad ties like in the movies, like runaways or hobos on an adventure. Sharp gray and white rocks lay between each tie and covered both embankments. Reagan could feel the edges through the soles of her boots when she misjudged a step.

"The crushed rock is a fairly new and welcomed addition," Cass said. "There used to be lots of mud and erosion that made it hard on the three-wheeler when it rained or during spring melt. The government finally acknowledged that seven families lived out here over the next several miles. Some families have young kids, so they decided to enhance our access just a bit. We may not have a road, but now at least we have rocks."

.   .   .

"How did you haul in all the supplies for building the cabin and all of your stuff?" William looked at the ground to time his footsteps; it wasn't easy walking.

"We hired a large flatbed boat for the big things like the furniture. Our cabin is right on the river. The first winter we moved a lot by snow machine. We cut the logs right from the land we wanted to clear. Paul hired two guys to help him, and a neighbor had a tractor that we used for a week or so. It went amazingly well."

"A neighbor?" Reagan's voice showed surprise.

"Yeah, about two miles up river. There are some fairly good paths cut through the brush for a big vehicle like a tractor. A couple of families have been living out here for over twenty years."

The railroad tracks turned onto a railway bridge over a fast moving river. The water was a thick gray clay color. Two twelve-inch planks ran along one side of the tracks, with a rope handle on each side. Reagan tried not to look down at the water rushing about fifty feet beneath her feet. Cass continued talking as she walked gingerly across, but the sound of the rushing water drowned out her words.

Once on the other side, Reagan realized that Paul must have driven the three-wheeler across the bridge too. He was out of sight.

The three of them walked on for about two miles. Reagan took her sweatshirt off and tied it around her waist. The sky was a brilliant blue. Mountains were visible off to the east. Paul was sitting at a break in the woods near the side of the tracks, waiting for them.

"There's the driveway, so to speak," Cassandra said. "You may want to put your sweatshirt back on and put your hood up. The mosquitos can be terrible in here. We have about half-a-mile to go." Cass pulled a crumpled fishing hat from her back pocket and pulled it down over her hair.

Paul had a big smile on his face. "What do you think so far?"

"Great," William said. "That river is beautiful."

William and Paul had grown up together in northern Minnesota. They knew about beautiful lakes and wilderness and spent their summers camping and fishing. Golden boys at Ironwood High School, Paul went on to Harvard, and William went to Northwestern.

There was a path about four feet wide through the dense forest just the width of a loaded-down three-wheeler. The forest floor was thick with plants; ferns and small trees grew up to the edge of the path.

They followed Paul, walking fast to keep the mosquitos at bay, finally jogging the last half of the way, swatting and talking the entire time.

Reagan looked around when they reached the clearing. It was a good four acres of completely cleared land in a huge circle. A log cabin stood in the middle of the clearing. Colorful pansies and poppies grew along the side of the house. The entire clearing was covered in short grass. It was a remote paradise. A postcard from the edge.

"My God, it's beautiful." Reagan whispered.

"Well, thank you. We think so." Paul beamed.

"I can't believe you have a lawn!" William shook his head. "Who mows this monster?"

"We've got a big riding mower. We figured it was a necessity. The lawn keeps the mosquitos way down and discourages bears and other wildlife from getting too close."

Bears. "What kind of bears?" Reagan tried to make her voice nonchalant.

"Grizzly, brown, black, you name it." Paul slapped at a bug on his cheek. "Did you see the fresh scat on the trail? We scared some bear off."

"No, I guess I missed that." Reagan smiled and focused on the scene before her: the cabin, the circle of green, the outhouse near the edge of the cut grass. Close to the dark wall of trees.

"This must have been a hell of a job." William shook his head. "Just clearing the land."

"Yeah, well, I wasn't doing any eight to five, remember? It took almost two years to get where we felt okay about staying up here full time. I hired some help. I'm glad it's as far as it is."

．．．

THE CABIN WAS rustic but very comfortable. A generator provided the electricity and a hand pump outside provided fresh water. There was a loft that was Paul and Cass' bedroom. The living room had a futon sofa for company.

After unpacking and getting settled in, Cass made some strong coffee which they sipped while eating fresh baked bread. It was June sixteenth and fifty-two degrees.

REAGAN FINALLY REACHED the First Avenue exit from the freeway. Traffic was crawling along due to an accident near the Basilica. It looked like a couple of cars and a motorcycle. Reagan looked away as soon as she saw the motorcycle. She watched the other shoulder of the road, as police motioned her around. Thirty minutes behind schedule, she called her office and spoke with her secretary. She did what she could over the phone. Checked her messages. William would be late tonight. Some client in from Denver. Dinner and a Timberwolves game.

MOST OF HER memories of the trip to Alaska were pleasant ones. She sorted through them when she wanted to distract herself from the bear story. She remembered evenings when they all cooked together while drinking wine and listening to music. Then they sat around the fireplace, sipping brandy, discussing politics and books.

The place was so quiet at night it was almost eerie, as if she was sleeping in some kind of vacuum. She slept hard and woke each morning to the smell of coffee and breakfast cooking.

The air was clean and crisp. She let the city fade slowly and quietly into the edges of her memory. Minneapolis was a beautiful city, but it was a city with all the chaos and confusion of any large metropolis. It was where her life and work was, where her lists and her calendar kept track of her days; she had needed a vacation more than she realized.

REAGAN RETRIEVED pleasant memories of the trip, but then unexpectedly and unannounced, the image of the bear climbing up on to the roof of that house came back and slapped her across the face. A cold, stinging sort of pain. A surprise attack that closed her throat, made her fight for air. She felt an uneasy anxiousness then, a feeling that pervaded more of her days. The feeling hampered her sleep, took the edge off her appetite. Things didn't feel like they were working properly. Her life felt somehow threatened, as if things were about to drastically change.

Reagan was back on schedule by eleven o'clock. The depositions were in her office. Things were moving along by eleven-fifteen; she had a late lunch a little before two.

She ate the take-out salad at her desk, reviewing the latest draft of the Skylar summary judgement motion, making notes in the margin.

THE LAST NIGHT out at the cabin, Paul told the story about the bear. They were grilling salmon outside, and he got to talking about how he went down to the Kenai River every fall to go salmon fishing, and how somebody always saw a bear or two, and how the papers kept a running account of who got in a bear's way and got mauled. In the wrong place at the wrong time.

"But the story about the young married couple, I tell you what, I heard that story the year Cass and I moved up here full time. It was enough to stop and make me think. That's why I always carry a gun now. Usually this forty-four Magnum pistol."

He reached into a holster at his waist and got out the gun Reagan had asked about on the first day. It looked like a TV gun.

"Doesn't look big enough to kill a bear," Reagan said.

"Not unless you aim well and hit him in the right spot. Preferably a couple of times." Paul shrugged. "I'm okay with a gun. I tell you what, I feel more comfortable with it than without it."

"So what about this bear climbing on a house," William asked.

Reagan had hoped they would just skip the details.

"Well, this young couple had just moved up here. They had built a cabin, sort of a story like us." Paul took a drink of beer and checked the salmon on the grill. Delicious barbecue smells swirled around the foursome. "They lived in a tent a couple of summers while working on the place, and the guy said they'd never seen a bear, not anywhere near the cabin anyway, but this big brown bear comes sauntering into the clearing while they are outside. They are out in back chopping wood, and he has an axe but no gun. The bear gets pretty close before they see it. They had been repairing some shingles on the roof, so they had this ladder there.

"I guess they figured they had a better chance than trying to get into the house. Anyway, they climbed up on that roof and pulled the ladder up after them. Well, the way I heard it, the bear went kind of crazy, must have been starving or something, but it went around the cabin, broke windows and broke the door down, went inside and ransacked the kitchen, eating whatever it found. But then it didn't just leave when it was full; it came back outside and circled that house grunting and making a hell of a noise. By this time, they had been up there for hours. I guess the guy must not have had a gun, but anyway, he decides to make a break for it." Paul paused.

"They had a boat tied up down by the river. They were on the water just like we are. So he runs for the boat to go and get some help from a neighbor. He said the bear had to have weighed nine hundred pounds. When it stood on its hind legs, it could claw at the shingles at the edge of the roof. We're talking a monster."

Cass shuddered, looked at the grill where the fish sizzled, and then up at the roof of her own cabin.

"And?" William leaned into his question.

Reagan wanted the story to end. Wanted the bear to fall down dead of a heart attack. Wanted it to be a joke with a bad punch line.

Paul continued. "And the guy just got out into the current of the river when he saw the bear make his way up the chimney like he was climbing a tree. Got up on that roof and mauled and killed that woman right in front of her husband's eyes."

Reagan turned away; she wanted to walk away, but that would mean getting closer to the trees, closer to the dark wilderness. She closed her eyes and tried to forget what she had just heard. It was no use.

The group was quiet for a minute; there was nothing to say that would top the powerful image of the end of the story. "Did that really happen?" Reagan brought herself to ask.

"It really did," Cass said, sounding bewildered by it all over again.

That night in bed in the living room, Reagan kept looking from window to window in the cabin. Because the summer nights were like dusk until one o'clock in the morning, she could see each tree's outline, could imagine every creature coming in search of food.

William slept hard, snoring and twisting the blankets around his pale, toned body. The next day they headed back to Anchorage, back to the city of the north and the first part of their journey home.

REAGAN PLAYED her messages back again. William would be late. She thought perhaps she should call his office to be sure she had gotten the message right. Something deep inside of her cracked a bit, like old porcelain; a web of fissures was forming, fine dark lines that compromised the strength of the whole. Would William ever have an affair? He certainly had the opportunity; his firm was teaming with bright women who obviously admired him. Reagan was no fool. She knew the motives of young, ambitious women. She had been one herself not that long ago. She and William needed to sit down and talk. Take some time for each other.

She put the finishing touches on the Skylar motion and called in a young associate to take it through the final stages. Let her see the final copy before it went out. The motion may or may not go well. It was hard to guess these days, but she'd done what she could. This sort of thing just went by the numbers.

By seven o'clock, she had the stack on her desk back to a manageable size. She reviewed the next morning's appointments. As she got into her car in the parking ramp below the building, she wondered if the traffic would be cleared. It was snowing lightly; the roads could be slow. Pulling onto the entrance ramp, she thought about the bear again. It was when the quiet surrounded her that she could not escape. And always, when she thought about the bear, her mind drifted to the woman. The woman clinging to the roof of her home, looking off toward the river where the man she loved sat, a look of terror on his face. He knew, just seconds before she did, what was climbing up to get her. He knew and he screamed for her to jump and make a run for it! But the water sounds and wind carried his voice away. And by the time she saw the horrific beast, and they looked eye to eye, she knew that there was nowhere to run.

And, Reagan thought, there was nothing, nothing she could do.

4

FIRE

She didn't really believe it was happening, believe that it was her house enveloped in orange flames like a jack-o-lantern laughing crazy. There was nothing there, nothing but the heat on her face, the November night on her back, and the sounds of others getting involved.

She had arrived about twenty minutes earlier, or maybe it was hours. It was difficult to measure the time it took to watch a part of your life burn away. Janet only knew there were more people milling around now and less of her home still standing.

It was her last night class of the quarter. The students wanted to go out for a beer to discuss anything but final papers and essays, anything but Sexton and Plath and their place in contemporary literature. They went to an Irish bar on Seventeenth. She always enjoyed talking with the students, shedding her role as professor, instructor, keeper of the grades. She felt a sort of satisfaction at the fact they invited her on these outings, asked her what music she listened to, what her favorite books were. And sometimes she would ask them questions, quizzing them selfishly to get inside the minds of those ten years her junior to find new material for characters in her work, ideas for her poetry.

When older people asked her what she did for a living, Janet said she was a teacher. If they were younger or her own age, she said she was a writer. It had something to do with responsibility and acceptance, with reality and art, and Janet Harris knew those boundaries well. She liked to think both parts of her could coexist happily, could function in her world as one, and yet, she often found herself apologizing. She grew up in a small midwestern town, wore braces when she was in high school, and learned to play the piano only because her mother had always wanted to learn. She craved independence and moved out when she was seventeen to begin college.

Nothing about her college education seemed unusual; she followed the normal paths. She learned how to fall in and out of love, wrote papers on the symbols in Stephen Crane's stories, worked at a bookstore off campus, and had her first poem published in the college literary magazine.

Standing with her hands in the pockets of her jeans, she made a mental list of what was slowly melting beneath the heat a few hundred feet away. The first thing that came to mind was her collection of vinyl. Joan Armatrading was on the turntable; she was sure of that. She had listened to the album at dinnertime before class. Janet thought about her smooth, deep voice, her potent lyrics, gone. And there was her collection of reggae and jazz, her folk music from the Greek islands, her Springsteen and Neil Young. All gone.

Her plants. The rubber tree would go first. It was sensitive to heat and required special care. The light and water had to be just so. The fig tree, the palms, the ferns, her spider plants. . . like one fast glimpse of the desert, the water would be too late.

Words. She imagined she could hear her books crying, screaming in pain from the intense tongue of the fire, the barbed flames eating away at their pages. Her desk was filled with new poems, files containing the years of her life in words, in stanzas, with no memory clear enough to replace them.

Red flashing lights circled the sidewalk in front of her, bouncing off her sleeves and open car door, bouncing across the strange faces and neighbors' homes. Pale leaves still clinging to the trees caught the color and looked like carnival lights strung down the boulevard.

The night was filled with light, filled with the bleeding tone of wood gone mad.

The world on her city block crackled with the fire's energy: people gasping as embers from the house drifted into space, children playing tag in the crowd, water hitting the roof in waves, windows shattering, rafters falling in, and someone crying ever so softly.

Janet had just refinished the rocker in her living room. She bought it at a neighborhood rummage sale for five dollars and spent all summer sanding and staining. She liked to sit in it at night and watch the sun set through her picture window, as the neighborhood changed clothes from afternoon to evening, and the world reshaped itself. The chair made a comfortable sound on the wood floors, a low creak with its movement. The bones of the arms fit her bones exactly, the back was a comforting friend. It was her favorite place, that chair, in that spot, in her house.

IT WAS HER FIRST HOME, her first freedom from small apartments and leaky faucets. Her parents saw it only once while on vacation. They drove up and stayed for a weekend. The three of them grilled burgers in the backyard and played Monopoly, drinking wine late into the night. Janet felt like she was on a new level with them, and it was comfortable. She felt more at home than ever in her life.

The roof collapsed, bringing down a part of the south wall with it like charred dominos toppling one after another. Firefighters in their yellow suits and masks ran back and forth, calling out in muffled voices. The image of the masks reminded Janet of insects, the eyes and mouths of something much smaller.

Finally things began to slow. When the water was louder than the hiss of the flames, the crowd grew bored and began to thin out, to go home. A firefighter walked through the crowd asking questions, inquiring about the owners of the house, taking notes in a small black note-book, but Janet could not move, could not volunteer the information he wanted, could not remove her hands from her pockets, her eyes from the picture window frame, her heart from somewhere within its gutted interior.

She thought about riding her bicycle when she was ten, riding down the path to the schoolyard with the huge paved playground, riding circles around the swings, circles around the slide, circles around her tenth year. She thought about building snowmen, learning to cross-country ski, learning to write sonnets. She made a list of the groceries she needed, the clothes that had to be dry-cleaned before winter, the birthday card she must address and send out.

. . .

NEXT WEEK GRADES WERE DUE; it was always a busy time. Her living room floor would be covered with piles of papers and old tests. She liked to get the full view of a student's work; it helped give her perspective in her grading.

Perspective, she thought. There was a need for that now. The firefighter was talking to a woman close by, sweat rolling down his face from the night. Janet's mind raced with questions. When would the smoldering stop? When could she return? When would it be safe to look up close for anything that remained stronger than the fire?

Shivering slightly, she noticed the cool sharpness of the night had returned. She smoothed her hair and brushed her hand across her damp cheek. There would be snow soon. Perhaps she would go home, to her parents' home, for Christmas. She had so enjoyed their last visit.

5

WHITE PAINT

After untying the bandana around the right leg of her jeans, Sam rang the buzzer. She grabbed the door, maneuvered her bike in through the cramped entryway and up the flight of stairs to her best friend's apartment. The hallway smelled of spaghetti sauce and stale cigarettes.

"So he's getting it somewhere else. Big deal," Leah held the door open. "We're not married, right? It is the nineties, after all."

Sam leaned her ten-speed bike against the living room wall. Leah smelled like booze. It was not a surprise. "Tell me the whole thing." Sam sat down on the couch and pulled off her hooded sweatshirt.

Leah shrugged. "Simple. Darin didn't come home last night. Ten o'clock this morning, I get a call. He says he got drunk, stayed at a buddy's house. Then this woman gets on the other line, you now, not knowing anyone was using the phone, and when she hears him talking says, 'Sorry Darry.' I mean Jesus. Darry? He says it's the guy's wife. Yeah, right. And he'll be home after some meeting at his office."

"And is that when you started drinking?" Sam looked at the clock. It was one-fifteen.

"Don't start on me, Sam. Didn't you hear a word I said?"

"Sure, and I want to talk about it. Let's go for a walk and get some air."

Leah sat on the arm of an easy chair directly across from Sam. "Have I ever told you that you can smile at some of the worst times? Have I?" She flashed a fake smile, lifting her chin high.

Sam looked at her fingernails. "Yeah, maybe once. Okay, twice."

"You're so damn happy all the time."

"Look. I didn't come over here for this. I know you're mad at Darin, but don't take it out on me. If I smile at the wrong time, I'm sorry. I came over here because you called and asked me to." Sam turned toward the window and twisted a strand of hair around her finger.

Leah poured something down the sink. The two women had a history. They grew up together. They learned how to smooth over rough edges, and they both had seen rough edges. Sam turned around and said, "How about some scrambled eggs? I'll make you some tea and you can take a quick shower. I'll even squeeze some orange juice."

"Help yourself, Betty Crocker. So you think I need a shower, huh?"

"It couldn't hurt. Maybe it'll give you a lift." Sam headed for the refrigerator.

"Some lift. If he comes in, keep him here. I have a few questions for him."

Sam began cooking. Acting out of habit. If someone is upset, you give them some food and hot coffee. You listen and listen and apologize for them. Don't worry Mom, it didn't wreck anything. I can probably sew it back together. The shirt wasn't that great anyway. See Dad, you didn't hurt her. She'll be okay, won't you, Mom? Come on, I'll call Gran and tell her it's still okay to come over. It's all right. I'm okay.

"FEELING BETTER?" Sam asked.

"Define that." Leah wrapped a towel around her wet hair.

Sam sat on the kitchen counter, eating a piece of toast. "Well, maybe it really was a wife. I think you at least have to hear him out."

"But Darry? What about that?"

"Maybe she didn't know his name."

"And if he's lying to me?"

"Move out."

Leah used her fork to push the eggs around on her plate. "Would you?"

Sam turned on the faucet and pulled out the rinse hose, spraying the dirty dishes in the sink. "I think so. I don't know. I mean, when I first started seeing Eric, he was still seeing what's-her-name. And sometimes I thought about him lying to me when he said it was over between them." She paused. "It always sounds easier when it isn't you."

Leah dumped the cold eggs down the disposal and patted Sam on the shoulder. "Thanks for the protein, lady. I feel better already. I suppose he'll be crawling in any time."

SAM JUMPED down from the counter. "I'm riding over to the art institute to look at a new show. Call if you want to talk. I'll be home by six."

"Forgive me if I forgive him?"

"Yeah. Just let him know he doesn't deserve it."

A COLD WIND snaked in around the neck of her sweatshirt as Sam rode towards the museum. The gusts brought dead leaves sailing down around her. Everything was molting, discarding color for the brown skin of autumn. Forgive me. She had suspected Eric wasn't being up front with her when he said it was over with Angela. But believing was easier then, so she learned how. Things grew deceptively simple.

Inside the museum, she allowed her heart to slow down. The biking had been hard work, facing the wind. Her face felt flushed. Tying her sweatshirt sleeves around her neck, she walked along holding an empty sleeve in each hand. Sam was a visual artist. The museum was where she sorted things out, lost in the framed worlds on white walls. The bright lights and white tile floors rebounded energy back and forth; she stood right in the middle and soaked up the charge.

ON HER WAY HOME, Sam stopped at a paint store and bought a gallon of white paint, a roller, and a couple of brushes. The landlord said if she ever painted she could deduct it from her rent. The living room had scotch tape marks and finger prints everywhere. Most importantly, it was Saturday night, and the hours stretched out in front of her like an empty airstrip.

Sam piled the room's sparse furnishings in the bedroom, collected all the artwork, and covered the floors with newspaper. She put the stereo in the kitchen and pushed up the volume. Reggae music filled the small apartment as lamps without shades cast curious shadows up and down each wall's face.

Drinking beer from the bottle, Sam moved with the music, bending her knees, keeping the white paint even, the strokes consistent. She was introduced to Bob Marley's music the year she studied at Bristol Academy in London. The white paint reminded her of the Easter holiday she spent in the Balearic Islands, one of Marley's old haunts. Whitewashed houses dotted the hillsides of Ibiza. She spent her time biking in the mountains, sketching the village plazas, dancing in discos at night.

Sam stepped back from the wall, remembering that long beach in the haze, the faceless man, and the sand. She felt the familiar pangs of guilt; the same lines ran through her mind over and over again. You drank too much. You should have known better. You should have known he was lying. You should have waited for your friends.

She had wandered out of the open air disco, looking for a friend who was studying with her at Bristol. The man grabbed her arm and headed towards the beach. "Where's my friend? I said I'd meet her here."

Sam remembered his choppy English. "You friend right down here. I bring you to her."

Before she knew it, Sam was lying on the sand, the man pulling at her clothes. Her head suddenly cleared, conscious of what was happening. "I want to dance. Dance first."

She couldn't remember his face. Just the hands pulling at buttons and zippers. "No. We do it now."

Sam ran her finger down his cheek. "I think we dance once. Then have lots of fun." She forced herself to kiss him, reaching her hand behind his neck. Her stomach heaved. "You and me dance, yes?"

The man released a low gurgling laugh. "Me and American woman dance. Okay. We dance."

SWALLOWING the last of her warm beer, Sam stepped back and looked at the white wall. "It never happened," she said. The words had been said before. "You used your head, and he didn't hurt you." But listening to her own voice, Sam felt his dirty tongue pushing into her mouth, felt the heaviness forced on top of her. The hurt was a deep mystery, a mixture of sadness and shame.

The three remaining walls looked dull gray in comparison. She put on a new album and started on the second wall. Leah would have to make up her own mind about dealing with Darin. Sam looked at the clock. It was eight-thirty. Leah would have called if things had gone badly. They were probably eating dinner out and making up right now. Fight then make up. Fight again. Sam knew all about it. She'd grown up in the middle of the ring.

She remembered the piece at the museum of the woman with four eyes. Each eye looked like it belonged; there was nothing unusual about the woman's face. Maybe she could see how things were, maybe two eyes were for looking back at the past and the other two were for everything else. Sam thought about that woman, eyes the green of peacock feathers looking out at her, looking back at an old lover, looking at poppies in a field, the reds so vivid you would swear they were beating hearts.

6

STORM

S now kept falling, over nine inches in the past twenty-four hours. Samantha invited Gary over for dinner. They had planned on going out to a movie, but many roads were impassible. Gary had a four-wheel drive, and Sam's apartment was near a snow emergency route. He suggested stopping for some wine and a couple of steaks and fixing them at her house.

Sam spent the day cleaning and baking wheat bread. She sat down on the futon that served as a couch, looking around for stray laundry, old letters, private artifacts. She wasn't used to much company these days. The apartment was crowded with plants and pictures. Photographs clung to the woodwork frames of the doors: the cottage near Chepstow, her parents standing by the lake at sunset, her first ballet recital pose. Sam was an artist, all her matted drawings rested on the floor along the wall. She smiled.

"Alex, this place is starting to look like a personal shrine. Now what are we going to do about that?" She bit her lip absentmindedly, pulling the dog onto her lap. The past clung to her like a child.

Midmorning, Sam bundled up and took the dog out for a little exercise. He floundered through the drifts in the yard. The snow was well past Sam's knees and near her waist in places. They stayed out about fifteen minutes. It was cold; the windchill was thirty below.

Gary knocked at six-thirty, stomping snow off his boots at the bottom of the stairs.

"Hey, Gar," Sam smiled. "How's the California boy doing tonight?"

"God, why did I move here anyway?" Gary asked, pulling off his boots.

"Too much sun causes cancer, remember?" Sam took the groceries as he reached the top of the stairs, giving him a kiss on the cheek. She put the bag on the table and linked her arm in Gary's.

"What a zoo. The roads they plowed are already filling back up. I bet we get a lot more by morning."

Alex was yapping loudly at the intruder. Sam scooped up the little dog. "Come on in."

Gary smiled and rubbed his cold fingers together, looking at Sam. She wore a maroon wool sweater and jeans. Grey sweat socks. The apartment was toasty and smelled of fresh baked bread. He pulled off his stocking cap and shook the snow from it. "You have a dog?" He sounded surprised and a little irritated.

"No. This is my cat. The dog's in the other room." Sam smiled. "Alex, meet Gary. Gary, Alexander."

"Charmed, I'm sure." Gary pulled off his down jacket.

"May I take your coat?"

Gary reached the parka toward her. "Thanks." Alex yipped, one single high bark. "Does he run on batteries?"

"He's protecting me. Don't worry, he'll calm down. Don't you like dogs?"

"Yeah. In cages, or on dog food commercials. They're okay on TV."

Sam rolled her eyes. "Well, he's welcome here." She put Alex on a pile of pillows in the corner of the living room and handed him a yellow tennis ball and an old canvas high-top. The dog began gnawing on the sole of the shoe.

"WINE?" Sam walked into the kitchen, past Gary, who was still standing at the top of the stairs. She perched the corkscrew on top of the bottle, watching the abstract doll raise her arms as she pirouetted, the sharp point clutching the cork. "I've made a salad. You want to broil those steaks?"

"Sure." Gary turned on the oven and rolled up his sleeves.

"I think some businesses may be closed on Monday," Gary said, breaking a long silence. "It doesn't look like it's going to let up." The steaks sizzled under the hot flame.

Wouldn't bother me. I could use the day off." Sam set the table and lit two slender candles. Alex came into the kitchen obviously interested in the smells of the cooking beef. Gary backed into him, causing a shrill yelp.

Sam picked up the dog and held him under her left arm, as she poured herself some more wine.

"So, how's your bus stop series coming?" Gary asked, holding out his glass. Sam drew people waiting around. Standing in line. Sometimes she worked in watercolor, but lately there was more charcoal. Rough, awkward lines. White space.

"Okay. I've been pretty busy."

"Have any shows planned?"

"Yeah, I'm trying to work up one for next fall."

"Really? Where?" Gary's voice marked disbelief.

"The institute might co-sponsor it. It's only in the planning stages, but we'll see."

"That's great."

Sam couldn't decide if his enthusiasm was genuine or feigned. She didn't trust compliments. She never had. He never seemed truly interested in what she did. It wasn't like her work was competition; he was a photographer. He had a show every year at the same gallery. But she was younger and a woman. Sam figured that probably mattered.

"Yeah," Sam said, rolling the stem of her glass between her forefinger and thumb. "I'm looking forward to it."

The table looked beautiful: a white linen cloth, golden wheat bread on a board, a salad filled with loud color, hand-dipped candles and steaks. Alex had eaten his dog food and sat at Sam's feet, whining softly. "No, Alex. Now bug off. You've had your share."

"Jesus. Can't you lock him in the bedroom or something?" Gary waved his glass at the dog. "Or better yet, the bathroom. We will probably be using the bedroom later." He smiled, raising his eyebrows.

Sam felt her stomach tighten, her appetite disappear. She looked at the half of her T-bone that was left. Picking up the brown and pink meat, dripping with juices, she dropped it in the dog's bowl. Alex tore at it, his tail wagging with excitement.

Gary followed her with his eyes as she crossed the room. She uncorked another bottle of wine. They had finished the first bottle rather quickly, and both their reactions seemed slowed. She filled her glass and sat back down across the table from him. "What was that about?" he asked.

"Can't we start this again?" Sam asked. "We're having a nice dinner. This is a date...sort of. I mean, if you were allergic to him, I'd understand. If he bit you, I'd understand. But, well, if you just don't like him for no reason, well I guess," Sam paused, took a breath and exhaled with "it's too damn bad."

Gary dropped his fork on his plate. "Touchy." He stopped at that. No argument, no counter attack. He glanced into the dog's bowl. "It looks like we're done with dinner. Should we do the dishes now?"

Sam wanted to pull back. She didn't enjoy confrontation, and yet she had brought it on. "No need. I just throw them out the window when they get dirty." She smiled and put out her hand. "Friends?"

Gary took her hand, smiling, but shaking his head. "Friends."

"No need to even pick up the table, Alex will do that." She looked down at the dog, sitting next to her feet with the T-bone stripped of meat between his front paws, chewing on the bone. "He is good for something."

Picking up her wine glass, she headed into the living room and the stereo. She put on a reggae album and sat next to Gary on the futon. "This music always makes me warm." Sam thought about the last time. She'd said sure, why not. No good reason to say no. While they made love in his water bed, she was thinking about summer school at college, lying on an air mattress in the quarries. Afternoons spent being a part of the turquoise water. A lily pad.

"You ever been swimming in a rock quarry?" she asked, leaning her head back against the wall. Gary put his arm around her.

"I think so. They kind of give me the creeps though. All that rock wrapped around you. Like a deep bowl. I'd rather swim in the ocean. Or a pool. Better yet, floating down a slow river on a raft."

"I like the closed in feeling. This quarry I went to all the time in college was about forty feet deep. Crystal clear. You could see your feet when you tread water. Like white anemic fish swimming beneath you."

"I used to surf," Gary said. "Mostly we partied on the beach. California. Sun, surf, and tons of people."

"I'd go out there and be all alone. Kind of dumb, I know, cramps and all, but I liked it. Floating on that cold blue glass, feeling like I was being pushed on from the sky. Some hand applying just enough pressure. I don't know."

"Speaking of oceans, I have another shoot on the east coast around the first of the year. I was thinking you might like to fly out there with me, take a little time off from work and spend a week in Boston. We could drive up the coast."

"That would be nice," Sam said after awhile, her voice void of emotion. "God, I was glad to be getting away that August. Bound for Britain. I'd spend days out on the warm rocks, studying for my last summer classes, knowing I was leaving Minnesota and college and all of it. Finally getting out of the cramped apartments with parking lot parties. These no-mind football players used to bust their heads through the thin walls, drunk and numb, showing off."

GARY PULLED Sam's hair away from her neck, letting it fall back, a small strand at a time. "What do you have against football players?"

"Only everything." Sam pictured Boston. She'd want to go to the aquarium and watch the fish. He'd want to go to some gym and get a good workout or back to the hotel room.

"I don't think I could get time off from work. I already took some vacation, and I want to save some for summer. Anyway, I can't afford to take time off. And Bart needs the help."

"Yeah, I'm sure he doesn't mind having you around."

"What's that supposed to mean?" Sam asked. She had never said much about her boss.

"I've seen him. Beer belly, mid-forties. I'd bet ten to one odds he's lusting after you."

Sam leaned away from Gary, studying him. "Just because he's in his forties doesn't mean he's a jerk, Gary.

Besides, you don't even know him. What suddenly makes you so protective?"

"I guess I'm jealous of other guys looking at you," Gary said, pouring more wine. "Even if he is married. I care about you."

Sam looked at the floor. Gary had never even been in her house before. He didn't know she had a dog. They had been out maybe ten or fifteen times over the past year, and he was showing signs of territorial rights? The wine cast a curious haze on the conversation.

Sam held in a strong urge to giggle. "That's nice, Gary. I'm glad you like me, but I'm nobody's girl, you know. I mean, I was a girl when I was twelve, but since then I've gotten my braces off, moved to the city, and grown up. I don't see things that way. No license, no deed of purchase."

"Don't blow this all out of proportion, Sam. Christ, you're touchy tonight. I give you a compliment, say I care about you, and you've got me trying to purchase you at a slave auction."

"Ah, Gar. What are we doing, anyway? Aren't we just using each other for some company? We both like to go out, and face it, we're just convenient. Let's not kid ourselves."

"What are you trying to say? Look, if you're not in the mood to jump in the sack, say so. Jesus, I figure there's over a foot of snow out there. We're probably going to be here for awhile. I just thought we could enjoy it." Gary went to his jacket, which was thrown over the seat of her bike resting against the wall of the living room, and pulled out a pack of cigarettes.

"When did you pick up this quaint habit?"

"Get off my ass, Sam. Okay? I don't think it's funny anymore."

"Well, since we need to make the best of things, maybe you'd better go outside and see if that Blazer of yours will start because there's no smoking in this apartment. That will give you time to inhale the thing while the engine's warming up."

Gary dropped the cigarette on the wood floor and crushed it with his boot.

"You burn that floor and so help me."

"Enough, Sam. You want me to go, I'll go. I don't know what's gotten into you, but it was obviously not the right night for us to get together." He reached for his coat.

"Very perceptive, Gar." Sam broke a leaf off her jade plant and began fingering it.

"Can I have a kiss good night before I go out in that shit?"

Sam wanted to slap his face. She wanted to head out to the rock quarries and dive deep, breaking the mirrored surface, but it was all too much work. She closed her eyes and kissed him quickly on the lips, for the last time. "If you have any trouble getting out, let me know," she said.

Noticing the smile returning to his face, she added, "I'll come and help you push."

After he left, she went to pick up the kitchen. Everything felt dirty. The dishes had a thick film of juice and solidified fat on them. The smell of cooked meat and smoke held in the air. Two empty wine bottles stood on the counter. She lit the candles again to clear the air and started water for dishes.

Sam filled the sink with steaming hot water; the smell of the dish soap mixed in with the smells of the kitchen. She wore rubber gloves and washed everything, scrubbing the counters and table, scouring the broiler pan. The music had finished long ago, but she didn't flip the album. It was the wrong time for Marley, the wrong time for music at all. Now she could clean and get things back in order. She put the dishes away, put the plant back on the center of the table, and swept the floor. The work and the wine made her warm.

She pulled out a sketch pad but threw it back on the floor before opening it up. Finally, she decided on bed. Let the snow paint tonight. The transformations would be waiting for her in the morning. It was eleven o'clock. The phone rang.

"Sam?" It was Gary. "I just called to say I got home okay. The roads aren't really that bad."

He had softened. He sounded apologetic. All she could think about was saying she hadn't been worried, she knew he'd get through, he'd make the vehicle do what he wanted it to. There had never been any question in her mind. She heard herself say, "I'm glad, Gary."

"I'm sorry about tonight. Maybe it's the weather."

"Yeah, maybe." Sam didn't sound convinced. "It's late, Gary. Good night."

"Good night. I'll call you," he added.

Outside the snow fell in the circle of the street light. Except for a couple of parked cars, it was impossible to tell the street from the neighborhood lawns. Huge drifts curved from house to house like waves cresting and falling with the pull of a distant moon.

7

MADAM HEART

At seventy-two, she still kept the place dancing. Curtains in each open window on the second story caught the breeze and played against the screens. The yard was well tended, green and lined with lively flower gardens. Even the trees seemed sculpted.

The house was a huge Victorian; ornate upper story windows still contained stained glass. Long ago those on the main floor were broken either by neighborhood children and baseballs or a broom handle carelessly placed.

Inside, the polished wood floors and old furniture maintained their dignity. She had an old upright piano with yellowed ivories on one wall of the formal dining room. Huge piles of sheet music lay stacked on the top of the piano and on the floor near the long bench. The walls displayed prints, soft, rich colored advertisements for dance companies and theater openings, framed in the past yet holding the excitement of opening night.

They used to call her Madam Heart. Her full name was Madeline Estelle Heart, but people called her Maddie now. There was very little connection between the names, very little of her history that made sense as a whole. Her life hadn't taken all the right turns, according to some people. Neighbors used to ask politely why she ended up in a small town in Iowa, but then they never really knew Dwight.

She met Dwight Heart in Cleveland when she was seventeen. She was finishing high school and dancing many hours a day. He was in the Air Force, handsome and ambitious for a man of twenty-three. He liked to play baseball, go boating, and drink champagne. Three months after they met, he asked Madeline to marry him. She had never been in love before; there was very little to think about. She said yes.

They were married and moved to Chicago soon after Dwight was out of the service. Madeline had never been any farther west than Cleveland. The first winter was bitter cold. She was used to the moist air off the lake, but the city was new, the parks were foreign, and nothing seemed to generate warmth when she was alone. She liked recognizing faces, knowing what times the parks would be filled with people, knowing her world by its detail. It took time for Madeline to get used to the lack of familiarity, the new apartment, the long days.

Dwight got a job as an assistant manager for a new restaurant. He had an eye for business and management and soon found ways to increase their profits. Things seemed to come easily for him. He was well liked.

In those early months, they painted the walls of their apartment and refinished the old battered furniture. Dwight received a promotion after six months and took a second job downtown with another small restaurant. He started working long hours, but he was learning, and it seemed to be paying off.

Madeline adjusted to her new life. She spent most of her time in the parks, reading books or feeding the birds. She took dance classes several times a week and learned to cook. She felt there was so much to learn, so much information to weave into opinions of her own. The world unfolded before her. It was a new life, and Madeline wanted all of it. Her ambition showed. Dwight was proud of the way she charmed his associates at the social gatherings that seemed to be a bigger part of their lives now. He started wearing expensive suits and taking Madeline to the theater and fine restaurants several nights a week. He seemed to know everyone.

Dancing became more than a hobby to Madeline. She started working out every day; the studio opened at nine o'clock, and she was usually waiting on the steps. It was an addictive feeling for her, the way muscles warmed up and took over, responding to the pulse of the music. The concentration of movement filled her mind with energy. She wanted to learn new steps, new approaches to every move. She learned quickly; the mornings were never long enough.

The second winter they were in Chicago, she taught a beginning dance class at the studio. Because of her patience, the students worked well for her. She liked seeing them cross barriers they thought were impossible; the birth of new movement inspired her.

Dwight became a partner in one of the restaurants. He had more free time now, more time for big parties and weekend events with associates and their wives. He seemed to be working at so many things but said little about his business to Madeline. It became a forgotten topic at the dinner table or at night as they lay in bed talking. Instead, he always wanted to know what Madeline had learned that day, what interested her, what made her happy.

She often told herself that if there were ever a problem with the business or financing, Dwight would share it with her. She took the silence as a positive sign and didn't worry. They were good times.

One night, when they were getting ready to go to the

ballet, Dwight walked into the bedroom with two dozen roses and an opened bottle of champagne. Madeline first saw him in the bureau mirror, his smile, that look. He told her that she was the most elegant woman he had ever met. At that moment, to Madeline, it seemed like the world revolved around her. That was when he began calling her Madam Heart.

II.

IN WINTER, the house took on a shade of gray. In earlier years, there was always enough warmth. Dwight liked lights everywhere; he never turned them off when he went from room to room in the evening. Even the three unoccupied bedrooms always had a small lamp or two burning. Madeline grew accustomed to it.

Now, each fall contained rituals. She blocked off the entire house, except for the kitchen, the bath off the pantry and the formal dining room. First, she prepared the upstairs. She placed dust covers on the furniture, locked the windows, and moved all the plants to the dining room; they surrounded her piano like a small, indoor garden. Then she moved in the old velvet sofa from the library. She wasn't a particularly tall woman, and it slept quite comfortably. Her pictures of Dwight came from every room in the house: their wedding picture went on the piano; his first time out on his sailboat on a hutch in the corner; the time they went to the mountains on the kitchen table.

Maddie layered her clothes; it was the best way to keep warm. Heating was still expensive, even for the small area she afforded to live in. She saved wherever she could. Blankets hung over the double doors between the dining room and the living room to conserve the heat from her small space heater. It always pleased her when there was a large snowfall early in the season; it insulated things so well. The corners outside the bay windows collected huge, soft drifts that blanketed the house with a feeling of warmth.

After such a snowfall, she bundled up and went out to clear the walks. It was nice to be working and growing warm out in the white world. She loved the ice-coated branches of the trees and how they resembled crystal in the morning sunshine. She used to visit with the neighbors, the Denali's, after a fresh snowfall, but their house was empty this year. Maureen died of a heart attack last fall, sitting on the front lawn. Her husband was in the hospital. Some nervous condition, Maddie had heard. So now a service came and chewed up the snow with one of those big snowblowers and spit it out onto the lawn. It took ten minutes, maybe fifteen after a heavy snow, then they were gone. No conversation over the drifts. No exchange of daily news. It usually took Maddie until nearly lunchtime. Of course, that included clearing the bird and squirrel feeders, and it assumed that the snow had stopped falling. For an old woman who appreciated the look of a fresh snowfall, northern Iowa winters were beautiful but difficult.

III.

DWIGHT BOUGHT a second restaurant and things went well for a time, but Chicago seemed to be going through some hard times and the young businessman got restless. He never discussed the move, until he brought home two airplane tickets and suggested they fly to Des Moines and find a nice little town, buy a house, and settle down. Open their own restaurant. Start again.

The flight had been comfortable, as most things were in the Heart's lives. Dwight did not talk about the reasons for the move, and Madeline didn't ask, but she couldn't help wondering what secrets this man held behind his smile, his warm eyes. She wanted to be a part of his decisions, a part of the planning aspects of their lives, but instead, she felt like the dancing doll on top of the music box she had as a child. Tonight she was dizzy.

They spent a week driving around Iowa and found the house on Grange Avenue in the small town of Grace. It was a beautiful house and a quaint little town. On the flight home Dwight finally turned to Madeline for an opinion. "So, what do you think about the move? Do you like the house?"

Madeline was angry with herself that she had remained silent so long, angry that she had always followed someone else's lead. "I don't understand, Dwight. Why do you want to move? Why is this all happening so fast? I want to know why. I need to know why."

"Look, love. Things haven't been going so well in the two restaurants in Chicago. I have enough money left to open a small place somewhere outside of the city where the cost of living is lower. Chicago is a hard town." He looked out the window and then back at his wife. "You need to trust me. I love you." He ordered champagne and then they held hands while they slept.

Once home, Madeline agreed the old house was gorgeous. She would get used to living in a small town. In less than two months, they were moved. Dwight tried to fill in the gaps. Where there was no ballet, no live theater, they drove out to the river and watched the sunset. There were no fancy restaurants, no night clubs. He cooked at home and they began to read more.

After the restaurant was established, Madeline opened a small dance studio and taught beginning ballet to classical dance. For years the two lived on each other's energy, on each other's light, but the afternoon Madeline received the telephone call from the hospital, she was not prepared. Dwight died of a massive heart attack at the age of fifty-one. No warning. No reasons. Just a warm hand turned cold. As she left the hospital, she remembered the day he told her she was the most elegant woman he'd ever known. Roses. Champagne. A long time ago. Walking to her car, she fought for that elegance that comes with dignity, with grieving openly for the person who made her life a celebration.

The months that followed were a challenge. Madeline discovered that there were so many holes left in the world that Dwight had built around her. He had always looked so sure, so competent in his ventures. First, she discovered that his payments had lapsed on his life insurance policy. He was not covered. Then, the restaurant. Poor tax records, debts not paid, loans with high interest, people left angry with the man who had charmed her every day of her married life.

Madeline was not a weak woman. She faced the problems one after another and tried to finalize the life that was now so far out of reach. The restaurant sold quickly. She kept teaching dance for a time, but it had never made much money.

Over the years, things changed. Houses were torn down in her neighborhood, new ones constructed. Neighbors children grew up and left; the parents died or went to live in a small room where their meals were served three times a day. But Madeline's house was her own. She tended it and looked after its every need as if it were an ailing lover. New paint refreshed her spirits, and flower gardens dressed the lawn. She grew used to the silence of the nights, the bed with two pillows, the pictures of him on the walls. Madeline believed in allowing the seasons to take their course. She learned to adjust.

IV.

ON THE FIRST warm spring day, Maddie brought the house back to life. She started by removing the dust covers and washing or airing out the curtains and draperies. She opened the windows and let the fresh breezes cleanse the musty, still air. Plants were placed by windows in all the rooms where the sunlight was best. She put her wedding picture back on the big bureau upstairs, next to the four-poster bed she had slept in for over forty years. Dwight had picked it out and had it delivered as a surprise. He said he loved to see her smile.

Every small piece of furniture or linen that could be moved outside to soak up the clean, fresh sunshine was moved. The clothesline was filled for days, and every evening she began to feel more at home, more comfortable and queenly in her beautiful palace.

She dug up the small garden plots for planting, piling the dead remains of last years flowers near the garbage cans. The soil was good and black and warmed her hands in the sun-filled afternoons. Soon, small green arrows would force their way through the soil and stretch out into a world of color. The trees would blossom. Maddie eagerly awaited the first scent of lilacs that carried into the house on a young breeze.

When the weeks of opening were past, and the house looked as it had in years gone by, Madeline was happiest. People who thought they knew her, or who had an interest in the property, had been trying to convince her to sell it for years. A two-story, four-bedroom house was no place for an old woman, they said. But she never invited them in for tea, in to listen to her play the old piano, or to browse in the grand library with leather-bound books and maps of far away islands Dwight had hoped one day to visit. She never let them see the majesty of the old wood floors, the doors' carved artistry and the religion of the stained-glass windows still intact upstairs. She alone knew the music of grand memories.

On the best of days, she danced on the polished floors of the living room. Humming, slowly remembering the steps that matched the music's phrases, she twirled around and around the huge room. Madeline Estelle Heart had the smile of a young dancer on her face, an artist aware of the importance of timing. Slowly, she moved at first, stretching and reaching into every part of her body, until she could feel the familiar knowledge of muscles that were warm and ready to take over on their own, ready to dance to the music she heard.

8

THE END OF SUMMER

It was dark before Raven left the house. It wasn't until she was on the step outside and had locked the door that she realized it. She would have to go back in and pull the shades and put the small lamp on the end of the table by the window to give the impression that someone was home. She didn't want any trouble.

The fresh air smelled of cedar and pine. The lake was nearby, and a small breeze carried the sound of the waves lapping on the beach. A small garden near the end of the house was dry and browning. The soil was too sandy, and Raven usually forgot to water the slightly crooked rows in the evening.

Her car was hot and smelled of musty upholstery. An old navy Buick. After adjusting the mirror, she glanced into the glass and noticed her eyes but only for a minute.

They reminded her of olives, almost an edible green but certainly not attractive.

The gravel road threw dust into the vents. Annoyed that she had forgotten, she quickly closed them muttering to herself. On the main highway, she rolled down her window and dangled her thin arm out, resting it on the side of the car only after she was assured it was cool.

Craig would be home. It was Wednesday, and he wouldn't be bowling because of the tournaments. The only other possibility was fishing. He would be home. She would park in the alley by the hardware store. It was her way. He never knew when she was planning to visit because she didn't have a phone at the cottage. He liked surprises.

It was exactly a year ago this month he had asked her to marry him. It was her first summer living in the northern resort town. She remembered feeling dizzy, almost like someone had hit her. Craig was a good man. She thought maybe she had made a mistake by saying no. It was just too soon, or at least that is what she had told him. She didn't think about it often and rarely regretted her answer, but tonight was one of those nights. Perhaps they should talk about it again. It had been a year since the subject had been raised; she would be thirty-two next week.

Raven could see the lights from town; it was cooling off, and tourists would be going out to dinner or to have a drink. There weren't very many this year though, not like in the past.

She thought about Friday night. She would invite Craig to her cottage for dinner and make a big meal. Pot roast. Potatoes. Carrots. Maybe even buy a bottle of wine. He might not approve, but he did like surprises, and it would only be one bottle. She had not had wine since Christmas three years ago with her family back home.

Thinking about the possibilities for a nice quiet evening, she smiled contentedly as she drove onto Main Street. Mr Harrison was watering his flowers and waved. She waved back.

Turning into the alley, she parked near the brick wall and locked her car. Glancing at the reflection of her face in the car window, she brushed quickly through her hair with her fingers. It was growing long and getting bleached by the sun, but it wasn't long enough to behave well. She had never liked her hair; perhaps she would get it cut again.

Turning the corner near his house, she noticed his car was in the drive, and she smiled slightly; she was right. She looked through the sheer drapes, expecting to see him reclining in his chair watching television. Instead, he stood in the middle of the room with a woman. She was tall, though not as tall as Craig, and had long, dark hair. She was holding her hand over her mouth laughing at something. He took her other hand and led her out of the room.

Raven watched from the sidewalk without saying a word. After a long pause, she turned and walked back to Main Street. The neon light advertising LIQUOR was still lit on the storefront of Hanson's.

Inside, she could not remember which kind of wine she drank that Christmas, so she bought one bottle of red and one white. Carrying the cool bottles, she walked back toward Craig's.

Across the street from his house, she sat down on the grass under an old willow tree and twisted open the bottle of red. The day was darker now and considerably cooler. The wine tasted fruity and cold. It felt good on her throat. Across the street, Craig and the woman had returned to the living room. This time the lights were lower, and they were dancing. Raven recalled with a start that she didn't know Craig danced. She had never learned how herself. At school it had always seemed so forced. Warm gymnasiums and too many people.

The willow branches touched her cheek gently in the night breeze. Raven thought about high school, her days of silence and good grades. She finished the bottle of wine; and realized the couple had left the living room. Getting to her feet, she looked for a garbage can to throw away the bottle. There were none in sight, but she remembered that Craig's were at the end of his garage.

Crossing the street, she felt like she used to after carnival rides: disoriented, but certainly, certainly not intoxicated. Raven had never been intoxicated.

After quietly disposing of the wine bottle, she moved around to the back of the house. Walking tall, balancing the other wine bottle on top of her head, she imagined herself a woman drawing water from the village well in some far-off place. Raven stepped onto the deck which ran the full length of the house. Walking slowly, she reached his bedroom window.

The light was on, and the idea that the scene might upset her crossed her mind, but she did not want to go home and cry into her pillow. That was no answer, and besides, she didn't feel like crying. This way at least, she might begin to understand. She didn't really know Craig, and she was curious.

The light by the bed was on making it nearly impossible to see someone outside. A yellow hue filled the room leaving the impression of an old movie. Raven had seen his bedroom on a few occasions; in fact, she made the curtains that framed the window she was looking through. Craig and the woman were undressed and touching each other. Craig's large hands moved like a tanner inspecting a new hide, caressing and fondling. He seemed big, lying on the bed next to the woman. Raven had never thought about him as a particularly tall or large man, but he was.

She opened the second bottle of wine and sipped it, watching their every move carefully. Nothing else crossed her mind. High school was far away; even her cottage was a distant place.

The woman was not from town. Probably a tourist here for the week, or perhaps the summer. Raven didn't remember seeing her before. The two bodies moved like sand in the bed of a river, moving into each other as the currents required. Changing, the furrows on their faces growing tighter and deeper. Raven had never seen his face that way. It was as if he were trying to lift a huge weight, and it took his entire strength to keep it steady. The look interested her.

The woman was beautiful. Her dark hair curled around her neck and shoulders, capturing her. She had firm, tan legs and wrapped them around him, sculpting new pictures as she moved. She too seemed to be in a trance.

Raven had seen enough. On the drive home, with the bottle of wine in one hand and the steering wheel in the other, she considered what would have happened if she had gone into his house, let herself in with the key from below the mailbox, and walked quietly into the bedroom. She would smile, then slowly, deliberately, unbutton her blouse without speaking. Their surprise would be short, and then confusion would set in. Raven would slide her blouse from her slim shoulders, watching Craig's face the entire time. She would remove her bra, and then her skirt, and underwear. Naked, for the first time in his room, for the first time —she would smile at the woman and tell her it was all right. And then, she would touch him, watching them both carefully the entire time, moving slowly, deliberately, concentrating on the look on his face.

Perhaps she should go back. He liked surprises.

9

THE CRUEL WAR

Cora and Caitlyn Daneli sit on the long wooden dock throwing pebbles into the water. Cora, ten years old, sits near the shore where she can still see the rocky bottom of the lake beneath the pilings of the dock. She does not trust Lake Superior. She does not trust the power of its pull.

Caitlyn is only five and trusts everything. "I bet I can throw two of these rocks in the air and have them land in the same place. Make the same rings in the water, you know, those ripples. Wanna bet?" She looks up, squinting into the sun, her long red hair blowing around her face.

"I bet you could do it a hundred times and they wouldn't land in the same place once." Cora shakes her head.

"I'll show you." Caitlyn goes to gather more small rocks on the beach, and Cora reaches for her book. She is reading Pippi Longstocking and imagining she lives alone in a cave on a quiet tropical island. Pitching pebbles should keep her little sister busy and out of her hair.

There is a warm breeze. Maureen Daneli bangs the screen door of the cabin, a lawn chair in one hand and a magazine in the other. She is wearing shorts over a swimming suit and has on dark sunglasses. Her white legs are long and thin. "Girls, how are you doing? Shirley and I are going to have some iced tea; do you want anything?" She sets up her lawn chair, puts *Good Housekeeping* on the grass and heads back to the cabin. Cora looks up but doesn't answer.

Soon Shirley walks down from the next cabin carrying her own lawn chair. She is wearing a skirt and nylons with sandals. "Well, girls. Getting any fish?"

Cora looks up. Squints and looks out at Caitlyn, to see if there is even a fishing pole on the dock anywhere. She looks back at her book.

Maureen walks up holding two glasses of iced tea. "I told Ray that if he didn't get the car fixed this weekend we'd have to call a tow truck to come in here and get it, but you know how Ray is with cars. I hope the muffler holds until we get home anyway. The thing is starting to sound like a Sherman tank."

Shirley looks serious, looks away at a Sitka spruce in the middle of the small yard. A bird bath sits under it.

"Funny to have a bird bath right next to a lake," she says. "Always have thought that was odd."

"Sorry, Shirley. I wasn't using my head." Maureen reaches over and touches Shirley's arm. Cora is paying attention to the conversation, although it looks like she is reading. There is something about the Johnson cabin, Shirley and Garret Johnson, that intrigues her. Her parents use quiet voices when they discuss them at night. Every year for five years they have vacationed on the North Shore of Lake Superior, and every year the Johnsons have rented the cabin next to them. They're from Cedar Rapids. Home folks. He runs a hardware store, and she teaches nutrition at the vo-tech. This is the first year Jim isn't around. Fishing and playing beach volleyball with a bunch of kids he's met from up the shore a ways.

"What's the latest news?" Maureen turns the watch on her wrist around and around as she asks the question.

Shirley shrugs, "Nothing out of Washington. He's still MIA."

"Hey, Cora!" Caitlyn shouts. "I got two almost in the same spot. Look!"

"Well, he's in our prayers and so are you," Maureen says quietly.

"Doesn't count," Cora says. "Has to be right on top the other one. You got two sets of rings."

"I worry about Garret," Shirley says. "He can't seem

to concentrate anymore. Sits looking at the store's books at night and never even turns the page."

"Cora, look at this jewel!" Caitlyn is standing over her, barefoot and long legs showing beneath her cut-offs. She is going to be taller than Cora, no question. She holds an agate in the palm of her hand.

"Wow." Cora puts the book down. "May I look at it?"

"Sure." Caitlyn smiles and hands it to Cora.

"Well, I just can't imagine," Maureen says. "I really can't."

"Let's see if we can find some more of these," Cora says. "You go on one side of the dock, and I'll start on the other."

"Okay," Caitlyn's eyes are big. "Want me to go get a pail to put them in?"

"Sure." Cora looks at the dry rocks near the lake's edge, careful not to get too close to the water.

IT IS early evening on Sunday, and they are driving through Iowa heading home. Maureen dozes in the front seat. Cora and Caitlyn are best friends now, out of necessity and the close proximity of the back seat. Cora is teaching Caitlyn a new song. "The Cruel War is raging, Johny has to fight. How I want to be with him, from morning till night. I want to be with him, it grieves my heart so, won't you let me go with you…" Cora looks expectantly at Caitlyn.

"No, my love no." Caitlyn sings in her small voice. Then she looks puzzled. "I forgot the next part."

The car sputters and slows. Finally Ray steers it off the shoulder near what looks like an old school house. There are poles for a swing set out back, but no swings.

"Well, how about that," he says quietly, almost to himself, as he tries to start the car again. It moans and dies.

"I told you we should have stopped in town and had them take a look," Maureen says quietly, shaking her head.

"Oh, for chrissakes, Maureen. I think I know about as much about cars as anybody. Just give me a minute to peek under the hood."

"What's wrong, Dad?" Cora asks.

"Won't know till I take a look. Doesn't sound too serious."

Maureen sniffs and looks out her window.

Ray has his head under the hood for some time. "You women may as well get out, we aren't going anywhere for awhile. Maureen, will you hand me that map?"

The girls climb out of the back seat, happy to stretch their legs. "You see any cars coming you give me a holler, okay?" Ray says. "I may need a lift into the next town. So that's your job. Look out."

"Can we go explore this place?" Cora asks.

"Sure. You watch your sister. Maureen, we're going to need to get the suitcases out of the back so I can get at the toolbox. Looks like we got a problem with the connection and the brushes. You don't have a rubber band or two on you, do you? Maybe one of those binders you use for the girl's hair?"

Cora and Caitlyn find an old merry-go-round out behind the building. They give each other rides until they both feel queasy.

Maureen spreads a blanket on the ground, fixes some peanut butter crackers, and slices a few apples. She and the girls nibble at the food as Ray tries the car and it starts. "All aboard, he says, sounding cheerful. They grab the picnic and push it into the back seat, afraid the car will kill again, so they need to hurry.

Once on the highway, Maureen studies the map. "There's probably a station open in Simcoe. We'll get there in about half an hour."

"Oh, no need to stop now. It'll hold until we get home." Ray is confident again, his shoulders square after his success with the rubber bands. He laughs. "See the problem originally was a short in the starter motor. A couple of bare wires. Your fingernail polish took care of that just fine. I coated the wires to provide insulation, but then the problem was the brush springs lost their tension and were slipping. It should be just fine now."

"Wonderful, it's growing dark and you're trusting the car's mechanical ability to some nail polish and rubber bands."

"Nope. I'm trusting my mechanical ability." Ray looks straight out at the highway. "Twenty-five years," he mutters to himself, shaking his head. "I know about cars."

As LATE AFTERNOON turns to dusk, the landmarks become more familiar. They pass through town after small town where everything is closed up for the night. Ray drums the steering wheel. "Well, what's going on this week?"

"Not much." Maureen's voice is quiet and distant.

"I'm thinking about getting a new section of fence for behind that garden. What do you think?"

"Fine."

"How are the tomatoes coming along?"

"Fine."

Ray resigns himself to the highway, to the pavement and the dark shoulder. The occasional flash of a pair of eyes in the long grass of the ditch.

As THEY REACH the county line, Cora and Caitlyn are awake, on their knees looking out the back window at the stars. Caitlyn finds the Big Dipper. "The cruel war is raging," Cora begins.

Caitlyn joins in, confident of the words now. "Johny has to fight. How I want to be with him, from morning till night."

The two girls sing the song over and over again. By the time they reach Grace and can see their house, Maureen is singing too in a soft, reflective voice.

10

BARBIES

"I thought we was all going to play. You let me play that one time before." Caitlyn twirled her long braid around her finger and wrinkled up her face to make herself look mad.

"We were, not we was, you dope. And I never said you could play today, so get out of here." Cora stood up and put her hands on her hips. She was eleven, five years older than her sister. "I'm telling Mom if you don't scram!"

Ellen and Doreen sat on the cement floor arranging their little cardboard boxes and spool furniture for their doll's houses. "Ah, she can stay Cora." It was Ellen's house. She was an only child. She always gave in. "She can play with my Penny Brite doll."

"But she can't go to prom," Doreen said. "Penny Brite isn't old enough to go to prom." Doreen had a real

Barbie house and a car and twenty-seven outfits. She lived on the other side of Grace, over by the post office and the new golf course. The course wasn't finished yet, and there wasn't much grass, but they were building all the little ponds and bridges and planting trees. Someday she'd live near the country club. Doreen had a swimming pool in her own backyard, but most of the time she rode her bike over to Ellen's or Cora's, and they played Barbies in the cool basement.

Cora didn't like to swim anyway. "If we're going to play prom, I want the real Ken doll this time."

"It's my Ken. Why should I let you play with it?" Doreen looked at Cora, but Cora ignored her. Doreen went on. "I'm getting pierced ears this week. My mother said I could."

"You're going to let somebody stick a pin through your ear?" Ellen winced.

"It doesn't hurt, silly. They do it real fast and then you have earrings. Mom said I can have real gold ones if I promise not to lose them."

Cora sat back and thought about what it would be like to have pierced ears just like her Barbie doll. Barbie's earrings were little blue dots, but Cora's mom didn't even have pierced ears, so Cora probably couldn't get them either. Besides, she thought, the needle part didn't sound so good. She'd wait and see how Doreen liked them, if they got all infected and made her ears turn purple or something. "Well, if I have to pretend I have a date for prom again, I don't want to play. I'm tired of getting her all dressed up to go to a dumb old dance where I pretend she has a partner."

Ellen sniffed. "Maybe we could have a picnic and take them in the backyard."

"Hey, what about a swimming pool?" Caitlyn approached the group cautiously after standing back and listening. "We could dig a hole in the backyard and fill it with water, and then they could go to the lake and swim and have a picnic."

The three older girls looked at each other, finally Cora shrugged. "That might be fun. Might be boring though."

"I don't think we could dig a hole in my backyard," Ellen said. "My mom probably wouldn't like it."

"Well we could ask our dad," Cora said. "He's working in the garage."

"I'll bet we could dig back by the garden under that tree. I bet he wouldn't care." Caitlyn's voice was excited now. She was happiest when she was planning some new activity.

Ray Daneli was at the workbench taking apart a carburetor. He smiled when the girls came in. He wiped the sweat from his brow with the sleeve of his chambray shirt. There were big blue circles under his arms. "So how are my girls today?"

"We want a swimming pool, Dad," Caitlyn said. She

leaned her chin on the bench and looked up with big green eyes.

Ray laughed. "Oh yeah? Should we put in a guest house too, while we're at it?"

Cora rolled her eyes. "No. A little one. For our Barbies. I'd dig it myself out by the big tree where nothing is growing anyway, and I won't make a mess, and I'll put the shovel back."

"Now just how big of a pool are we talking here?"

"Just big enough, sir," Doreen said. "A kidney-shaped one like ours would be fun."

"Well, you take that spade out there and see what you can do. I need to put this thing back together, and then I'll help you out if you need it."

The girls all shook with excitement. They took a spade out around the garage to the shade of the old red maple. The Barbies were in their bathing suits, and Ken wore his terry cloth robe, since he would be the lifeguard.

AN HOUR LATER, long after the girls had given up on digging in the hard soil and gone in for Kool-Aid and chocolate chip cookies, Ray wiped his forehead on his bandana and stood over the girls resting in the shade of the maple. "So you want a swimming pool, do you?"

"Yes, sir." Doreen played with a strand of her long hair.

"I tried to dig it, Dad, but that shovel isn't any good." Cora stood up and walked over to the spot where they had tried to break up the dirt.

"Cora wouldn't even let me try, Daddy. I bet I could have done it." Caitlyn put her hands on her hips and returned the face Cora was making at her behind her father's back.

"Well, let's just see what we can do here." Within half-an-hour Ray had dug a kidney-shaped pool about three feet long, two feet wide and a feet deep. The girls were busy smoothing the sides so that no roots or lumps stuck out. It was hot, and each of them had dirt smeared across their faces. Ray was mixing up cement in a wheelbarrow when Maureen walked out to put a basket of laundry on the clothesline.

"Hey, Mom, look what Dad made for us! A Barbie swimming pool." Caitlyn jumped up and down. "It's going to be a real one with cement and fish and everything." Maureen walked up and looked at the hole then at Ray.

All the girls eyes were on her. They lay on their stomachs, their hands in the hole, patting against the sides. "Well, will you look at that." She smiled. "Looks like your father has another talent I wasn't even aware of. You want a cool drink, Ray?"

"Nah, I'm fine. Almost done here."

The Barbies sat in a row in their bathing suits, stiff,

thin legs before them and the girls sitting behind them, as Ray smoothed the cement up over the edge and formed a thick lip to the pool. "Now you need to leave this alone until tomorrow. By then it should be okay to put water in it."

The pool completed, the girls headed back to Ellen's basement to plan the next day's activities. "I'll have my mom take me to Woolworth's to get a couple of goldfish for the pond," Doreen said.

"I'll ask my mom if I can have some old washcloths to cut up for beach towels," Ellen said.

"We can make beach balls and a table and lawn chairs for by the pool," Caitlyn said.

"Out of what?" Cora asked.

"I don't know."

"You have to have an idea before you volunteer such a dumb thing." Cora said.

"Your guys' dad made the pool, that's enough," Ellen said. "I think that's enough."

"We'll think of something." Cora glared at Caitlyn. "Or I will. See you tomorrow."

For days, the girls sat around the small pond, tanning the plastic legs of their dolls, watching the small fish dart through the water. To cool themselves, they dipped their hands into the pool and splashed it up on their faces or smoothed it over their foreheads like holy water. They talked about Barbie and Ken and starting back to school in the fall. How Doreen's mother was going to have an operation and had to quit smoking. How it made her grouchy. They planned a sleepover in the backyard in Daneli's tent the weekend of the Fourth of July. Then they could watch the fireworks together.

Eventually, the water in the pond got too warm, and the fish died. Caitlyn found them belly up and buried them in a matchbox behind the peony bushes. The water got dirty and smelled a little, and mosquitoes swarmed around it. The girls weren't interested in scooping the dank water out and putting in new. By that time, the game had changed to something else. Barbie and her friends were skiing in Switzerland. As the summer passed, the pond dried up and filled with rain. Birds took baths in it, squirrels drank from it, but mostly everyone just forgot that it was there.

11

THUNDER

I was eleven the night we sat laughing inside that pup tent, telling stories and waving the flashlight around on the green canvas ceiling. Outside, the sky pulsed with silent flashes of light. The sort of lightning one sees on a hot Iowa evening. There was no thunder, no real threat of rain. The tent was in the yard behind my grandparents' old white farm house. A small garden with leaning hollyhocks and painted daisies separated our tent from the farm yard.

"I ate six apples once." Jake sat on top of his sleeping bag.

"At one time?" Caitlyn was wide-eyed. She's my little sister and was six at the time. Easily misled.

"Liar, liar, pants on fire." I pulled my gum out of my mouth and stretched it until it broke in two.

"Did too, ask Grandma." Jake squinted his eyes and

nodded toward the house. He had a butch haircut and a farmer tan from his baseball cap. Jake's my cousin and six months older. "It was right here in this yard. The apples were off that tree by the windmill. You just ask her. She knows it's true."

"Hope you got sicker than a dog." I smiled and popped the gum back into my mouth. Jake and I were in love with being mean.

"Mom says you ain't suppose to have gum in bed, Cora." Caitlyn sat with her thick red hair pulled back into a pony tail with one hand. "You know what happened that one time."

"Shut up, squirt, or you can just go in the house where babies belong. You want to sleep out here, you better stop acting like such a little tattletale." I blew a bubble and looked mean.

"Well, I ate 'em. All six of them. I didn't get a stomachache neither. Well, not a bad one anyway. Bet you couldn't do it."

"Bet I wouldn't be so D-U-M-B," I said.

There was a low rumbling sound off in the distance. "Hear that?" Jake asked. "Thunder. Means its going to rain like hell. We're going to get soaking wet."

"Oh, shut up." I unzipped the tent, tossed my gum, and had a quick look around. "Doesn't look like rain to me. And if you can't take a little rain, you better go inside with baby Caitlyn."

"You ain't suppose to swear, Jake," Caitlyn ignored my put down. One problem at a time.

"Rain don't bother me. You guys will probably be in the house before midnight. Girls can't take rain and the dark and stuff like that."

"What do you know about girls?" I asked. "You got a girlfriend? You like girls, Jake?"

"Not a chance. But I've got three sisters and they're all wimps just like you guys." Jake took off his canvas tennis shoes and started pulling out the laces.

"Seems to me we're sleeping in this tent too," I said. "I'd even make a bet about who will chicken out and go inside tonight. We'll stay, won't we, Cate?"

Caitlyn nodded. "I'm not afraid." She paused. "Well not much, that's for sure."

"What's that sound?" Jake asked. "I wonder if they caught that prisoner who escaped from the penitentiary last month. Some said he was heading this way."

"Real funny, dumb boy," I said. We climbed into our sleeping bags. It was getting a little cooler, but it was more for protection than anything else. Crickets chirped outside against the silence. "Is there really a bad guy out there?" Caitlyn asked.

"No, dummy," I said. "Jake is trying to scare us into the house. Don't worry about it. And you better shut up, Jake Anderson, or I'm going to tell Grandma and Grandpa you scared the pee out of Caitlyn."

"Ah, they won't do nothing." Jake slapped a mosquito. He was the first grandchild and could do no wrong.

"Then I'll beat the crap out of you, so leave her alone!" I laid down on my pillow. "I'm hungry. Any popcorn left?"

Jake handed me the paper bag. "What was that?" he asked.

"Jake, I said knock it off." I ate some popcorn. Caitlyn pulled the covers over her head.

"No, I mean it! I mean, I think I heard something this time." Jake was whispering now.

I stopped chewing long enough to listen. Not like I believed him or anything, but then I heard it too. A snorting sound, and bumping and moving gravel like someone was stumbling up the driveway.

We sat up and instinctively reached for each other's hands, trying to identify the sounds coming from outside the tent. The dragging gravel and snorting sounds grew louder. We could hear cows out by the barn bellowing and carrying on, but the new sound was close and getting closer. "Let's get the hell out of here," I whispered.

"No, I don't think we can. I mean... I think it's between us and the house." Jake leaned toward the zipper to look outside. My hands quietly searched for the flash-light. Caitlyn started to cry.

"It's okay, Cate. We're safe in here, don't worry. We'll get to the house, won't we, Jake?"

Jake pulled his head back in just as a loud bellow came from outside the tent, over near the dog house about fifty feet away. "Shit!" Jake turned to us. "You guys, it's a bull. It bumped into the dog house. His head was down and he ran right into it!"

"Shut up," I whispered. The bull was quiet, sniffing, standing still. We could hear its heavy breathing. The cows continued to bellow out by the barn. We sat still and tried hard not to breathe.

"I WANT GRANDMA," Caitlyn cried in a soft, terrified voice. I gently touched my fingertips to her lips and put my arm around her. The bull began to answer the cows, his angry bellows seemed even closer.

"Jake, do you think we can get out and run around the house the other way?"

"Bulls chase people," Jake said. "They're really fast." But this time all three of us were crying softly, trying not to make noise.

We heard the screen door from the house slam shut and then our grandfather"s voice. "All right, you old son-of-a-bitch! What are you doing in my yard?" The sound of his voice comforted us immediately, and we peeked out of the tent. Grandpa, in his underwear and T-shirt, stood holding a gun. The bull stopped and turned toward the sound. "Don't move, kids," he shouted. "It's going to be all right, but you got to sit real still and be quiet. Do not move."

A pickup truck pulled in the driveway and slid to a quick stop near the front of the house. A man jumped out and pulled a pitchfork out of the bed of the truck. The bull started to move toward Grandpa, but Grandpa darted out of the way. "God damn devil!" he shouted. The man got closer to the bull, stuck his pitch fork out, and started jabbing at him.

"Sorry, Joe. I don't know how he got out." The man shook his head. "Move over you crazy bastard, get home." The bull was bellowing and foaming at the mouth.

"Let's try to get him out into the barnyard area." Grandpa stood with his gun in one hand and a broom he'd picked up next to the steps in the other. "I got three grandkids in that tent over there."

"Jesus Christ!" the man said. "Look, we can try it, but if he's gotta go down, he's gotta go down."

Caitlyn and Jake and I stared out at the wild, muscled beast. He had foam dripping from his huge mouth, and he pawed at the ground.

Suddenly, Grandma appeared from the other side of the house, barefoot, in her robe, her gray hair in long braids. She ran straight to the tent. "Come on, kids. Hold my hand and run." We circled around the back of the house. I stopped on the front step and glanced over at the bull just as it smashed into the front fender of the man's red pickup. The metal folded in like paper. Grandpa handed his gun to the man, and he raised it to his shoulder and pulled the trigger before I could look away.

The bull sank to its knees and landed with a labored sound on the gravel next to the truck. It lay there, twenty feet from the front steps of the house. Grandma grabbed my wrist and gently pulled me inside. "Come on, dear, that's not for you to see."

"What happened, Grandma? What was wrong with that bull?" I looked into the living room. Caitlyn sat on the sofa. She was pale and still shaking, but she'd stopped crying. Jake stood there with his hands in the pockets of his jeans, looking out the living room window.

Grandma pulled the shades. She was a large woman and winded from our run. "He's the neighbor's Angus bull and he's blind. Must have got out and went kind of crazy when he heard our cows. Looks like he'd bumped in to some things on the way over here, and I think it made him mad." She sighed. "You kids all right?" She hugged each one of us and then looked us each straight in the eyes, holding each head in her soft, plump hands, as if the answer was held in our eyes. "Well praise God you weren't hurt."

"What was that sound?" Caitlyn asked.

"A gun," Jake said. "They shot it. Geez, was that thing ever big!"

"Is the bull dead?" Caitlyn looked to Grandma then to me. I felt sick to my stomach and looked away. Grandma sighed again.

"Yes, dear. I think it was in a lot of pain. Now it ain't. How about if we do something fun to take our minds off of it? I can't think anyone is going to sleep for awhile."

"Like what?" Jake asked.

"I've got some apples in the kitchen that would make a wonderful pie. We could peel them and bake one up. I even have ice cream. Do you suppose you could eat something that sweet this late at night?"

"I think I could," Caitlyn said earnestly.

"Great." Jake smiled at me. The adventure was continuing.

"Grandma, did Jake really eat six apples once?" I asked.

"As far as I can figure, he did, and he was sick for the whole weekend, but apple pie won't make you sick. Let's go to the kitchen and get started."

We sat around the gray formica table watching Grandma peel the bright green apples. The circular fluorescent light hummed above us. Flies and moths bounced against the outside of the screens. We heard Grandpa still out in the yard talking with the neighbor. We smelled cinnamon and apples and coffee.

"Grandma, what would have happened if you hadn't heard that bull and Grandpa wouldn't have come out to help us?" I ate a long, twisted peeling from the tart fruit.

Grandma paused for a moment, holding the paring knife away from the apple and titling her head slightly. "Then you probably would have saved yourselves and run around the house the way we did."

"How come?" I frowned. "I mean, we were afraid to do that and thought he'd chase us, and what if he'd of come over to our tent?"

"Well," Grandma wiped her forehead with the back of her hand, sighed, and began peeling again. "I don't think that was a possibility. You would have made the right choice if you'd been forced to. The human will works hard to survive. I think we was meant to make this pie tonight. It was the bull whose luck run out."

Now, years later, whenever I taste warm apple pie, I remember the process of that evening: peeling and slicing the apples, rolling out the crust, adding the cinnamon and sugar, then waiting in the warm summer kitchen. I remember more than a feeling of nostalgia, of an adventure turned brown at the edges like an old sepia photograph, more than the death of that bull. I remember how it felt, and how it tasted, and how it was to be alive.

12

THE SHOEBOX WALTZ

When Ray Daneli came home from work, Maureen could tell something was wrong. He parked the pickup next to the basketball hoop and kicked the tires as he walked by. He always kicked the tires, and his wife always watched from the window, but there was something else in his face today, something odd in the way his arms bounced limp against his sides.

"Good afternoon, dear." She spoke softly out of habit, not that the words held any meaning at all.

Ray let the screen door bang and walked past her, his face a vacant lot. He opened a cupboard door near the back of the kitchen and started pulling out cans and boxes from the shelves. Cheerios, peanut butter, soda. "Where the hell's that box?" he asked.

Maureen paused. "What box, dear?"

"Where the hell's that box?"

"Ray? Dear, what box do you mean?"

"Maureen!" he screamed. Then he turned to her. He was a tall, thin man. It was early September and a humid eighty-nine degrees. The top of his balding head glistened with sweat. Finally, his eyes focused on the woman with whom he had spent forty years. "Oh, there you are."

"What box are you looking for, Ray?"

"The shoebox, damn it. The one full of the receipts. I need the receipts. How am I suppose to run a business…"

"Ray, we don't keep a shoebox in that cupboard." Maureen quickly searched her brain. What he might have meant, what he was looking for, where it could possibly be.

"Well then, where is it?" Ray stopped short and stared at his wife, looking her in the eye for the first time.

"How about if you look in the hall closet. I'll look downstairs in your office." Maureen was always smoothing things over. A calm hand across white linen before placing the china on the dining room table.

"You hid it, didn't you?" Ray flushed at the thought. He walked over to the counter and placed both fists on the avocado formica, his back to her.

"Hid it? What are you talking about?" Maureen was shaking now. The kitchen felt hot and close.

Ray shook his head. "Jesus Christ" he said and walked out of the room.

Maureen went to the basement and quickly scanned the shelves for some box that resembled what Ray was looking for. She found nothing, sighed, and went to the washing machine to start some clothes. If she gave him time he would calm down and forget— forget what he was looking for, forget that she was there, and things would be back to normal. She sorted the light clothes from the dark ones. She placed her wrists on the white enamel side of the washer, cooling herself.

It was nicer down here she thought, dark and cool. This was her half of the basement. Laundry, a pantry, and racks for out-of-season clothes. Ray's desk was on the other half, sitting on top an old oval rug. A bare light bulb hung down from the open rafters. He worked at the desk nights, figuring out the books for his small auto parts business.

Maureen went back upstairs to peel potatoes for dinner. She reached the kitchen just in time to see Ray's red pickup pull out of the driveway. Things had been this way for months, maybe longer. She thought about talking to the pastor at church or one of her friends. Maybe even Ray's brother. But Maureen Daneli didn't know what to say. She didn't know what was wrong or how long it had been that way. She only knew that life's noose was getting tighter and tighter, and it was harder and harder to breathe. It wasn't a question of happiness or even love. She had forgotten about such things long ago. But her sense of normalcy and security were quickly dissolving, and that is what shook her the most.

It was Friday; the weekend stretched out before her. The best thing to do at times like this, she'd found, was to concentrate on daily things. Peel potatoes. Clean the chicken. Season it. Fry it. Make dinner. He would be back, and he'd want dinner, and he'd want it on time. Maybe that would be six o'clock, seven or eight-thirty, but when Ray Daneli opened the door to the kitchen, dinner was on the table.

WHEN THE TELEPHONE RANG, Maureen had the dinner dished up and ready to put into the microwave. She watched for her husband to drive into the driveway. She arranged everything on each plate as if it were a still-life, noticing color and texture. High school home economics. *Family Circle* food section. She held the phone in one hand and moved a crispy chicken leg slightly with the other.

"Mom?"

"Hello, dear."

"What's wrong?" Her youngest daughter's voice dropped at the end. She had grown used to picking up hints across the phone lines. Her hope that the conversation would be as pleasant as possible dissolved in her mother's whispering, defeated voice.

"Nothing. How are you?"

"What's wrong, Ma?"

"Caitlyn, I'm fine. It's hot here. I've been frying chicken. How's Greg?"

"Fine. And the boys are fine." Caitlyn paused, put both hands on the receiver to steady herself. "Mom. I was wondering, do you still have that little rocking chair of mine? You know, the orange one that Daddy painted? Is it in the attic?"

Maureen paused. "Caitlyn? I think so, I mean, why would you want that old thing now? The boys are much too old and...you don't have any little...."

"Yes, Mom, I'm pregnant."

Maureen was crying. A grandchild. A soft, innocent baby to hold in a flannel cocoon. A little girl to sing lullabies to while pushing soft, red curls from her damp forehead. A tiny hand like a walnut shell, to hold the hope of the whole world. Caitlyn was living with Greg and his two adolescent sons from a previous marriage. This would be her first grandchild. "Oh, Catie. I'm so happy. Are you okay? Is everything okay?"

"I don't know. I haven't told Greg yet. I wanted the first person I told to be happy about it."

"Well, what will you...." Maureen was shaking slightly now, looking out at the driveway as she spoke, half expecting Ray to pull in.

"I don't know yet. I want to get married, but we

haven't talked about that for a long time. I don't know what his reaction will be. It wasn't planned, but I'm happy about it, I think. I am happy. I just wanted to tell you and ask you to look for that old rocker."

"I will. And let me know what...." Maureen paused and looked around her kitchen.

"I'll call you after I talk to Greg." Caitlyn paused. "How's Daddy?"

Maureen did not want to spoil a lovely moment. "He's busy. Seems to have lots of work."

"Tell him hello for me?"

"Certainly."

In 1952, Maureen O'Duffy was working as a secretary at the local high school when she met Ray. She had a flat tire on the way home from work, and he stopped in his big gray panel truck and helped her change it. She was twenty-two with red hair and big Irish bones. Ray was twenty-nine and working for a local auto supplier. He changed the tire, gave her a complimentary pen with his business phone number on it, and asked her for her number. They were married eleven months later at the old wooden Lady of Light church in Grace, Iowa.

It was five years before Cora was born and five more before Caitlyn. Maureen continued to work. Her job had worn a groove in her consciousness, and she found the routine comforting. She took care of the daily attendance and absences. Every morning she knew who had the flu and who was out for a dentist appointment. When the girls were older, she drove them to school with her, and they all went home together at night. She enjoyed seeing them in the halls, talking with their friends, growing up before her eyes.

They had a good life. Ray got his own business, the girls did well in school, and everyone stayed healthy. Maureen didn't remember when things started to change or if they ever did. Maybe she didn't know what was missing because it had never been there. Maybe she was making too much of things. But these days, since the girls had left for college and gone off to have their own lives, she and Ray existed like roommates, telling a friendly joke now and then, putting up with annoying habits of the other, occasionally sharing a tender moment.

Ray drove up. Maureen put the food in the microwave and punched the time. She got the coffee and poured two cups at the table, thinking about Caitlyn's phone call. She wouldn't tell Ray until she knew for sure what Caitlyn was going to do. It was possible she would abort it, wasn't it? Maureen hoped not, knowing how hard it had been for her to get pregnant, how happy Caitlyn sounded on the phone. After all, Caitlyn was almost thirty, but it wasn't her decision. All she could do was wait and see.

Ray walked in, his hands nervously shaking a set of

house keys. Maureen said hello, carrying the two plates of steaming food into the dining room table.

"What's for dinner?"

"Chicken. It's ready." Maureen stood behind her chair smiling. Still a striking woman, five foot nine and thin. Long arms and fingers. Her hair was streaked with white, but wavy red wisps twined around her face.

"Did you find that box?" Ray looked past the table right into Maureen's eyes.

"No, Raymond. I have no idea what you're talking about." Maureen's shoulders slumped in defeat. The dinner was not enough.

"Yeah, I'm sure you don't. Trying to take my money without me knowing it. What else you got up your sleeve?"

"Ray, please. Can't we eat and talk about this later?"

"Eat? Why the hell should I sit down with you? Where's he eating tonight, huh? You got a boyfriend out there waiting to see you? Is that what all the hurry's about?"

Maureen stopped short. This was a new ballgame. It was as if something had snapped, all the small accusations, all the innuendo out in the open. Ray was shaking and shouting now. "All I do to make ends meet around here and what do I get from you? Maybe somebody else would appreciate the work I do."

Maureen looked at the telephone on the kitchen wall.

Maybe if she called his brother, he'd come and help her out. Calm Ray down. Help her figure out what to do next. She walked toward the kitchen.

The ironing board was folded up next to the telephone, and before she could reach for the receiver, Ray grabbed the board in his big hands and held it out at arms length. "So there you are, my lovely. Someone who will appreciate me. Someone who knows how to make a man happy. Shall we dance?"

Maureen was crying and felt like throwing up. "Ray, stop it!" she shouted. "Stop it right now, please. We'll talk. We'll get some help."

But Ray waltzed around the living room with the old wooden ironing board wrapped in his arms. He smiled and murmured at each turn. "Oh, baby, you are so good! Let's get that money and get out of here. Who needs a cheating wife? I can take my money and run. It's you and me. Maybe find some real happiness. Come on, give me a kiss."

Maureen pushed the numbers on the telephone for Ray's brother. Ray was oblivious to her now, twirling and humming in the next room. Maureen's fingers shook, and her stomach spasmed, as she listened to the hollow ringing on the other end of the line.

She counted to ten rings and then carefully returned the receiver to its cradle. It was getting harder to breathe. Without looking back at Ray, she walked out the side door to the driveway, letting the screen door bang behind her. It was beginning to cool off. Leaves on the old oak in the front yard whispered secrets in the evening breeze. Maureen looked up into the tree. There was a bird on one of the low branches ruffling its feathers, settling in for the evening. She didn't recognize the bird, didn't know its name or if it was native to the area. Maybe just passing through, she thought, headed for someplace else.

13

ALARM

My mother died of a broken heart in a crummy little town in Iowa. It was a humid night. The neighbor said she was out on the old wrought iron bench on the lawn and just sat there. Perfectly still. He was watering his rose bushes and finally walked over to see if she was okay.

Mom looked up and said "Ray doesn't love me." Then she grabbed her left arm. By the time the ambulance got there, they figure she was dead. Massive heart attack. She and my dad must have had one hell of a fight, because he lost it. Some kind of nervous breakdown. When a police officer come into the house to see if anyone was there, Dad was sitting cross-legged on the floor on top of an old, folded up, wooden ironing board. Like his body got tired of doing its job and just sat down in the middle of the kitchen.

They told me later that he just sat there and stared and didn't answer the officer when he talked to him, so both my parents were taken away with sirens and flashing lights.

I can almost hear the sirens. A week after I got back from Mom's funeral, the trailer house next to ours burned down. God, there were sirens and red lights everywhere. It smelled like burning plastic. I bet if you put your hand on the metal side of our trailer the next morning it still would have been warm. Nothing but smoke damage to our place though.

I was pretty nauseated, on account of I'm pregnant. Nine weeks. But I haven't told Greg yet, so I was acting like it was all that smoke. I haven't figured out what I'm going to do, so no use telling him until I get time to think this through. Greg's my boyfriend. We've lived together three years. Ryan and Daniel, his two kids from his first marriage, live with us. They're ten and thirteen, and it was really a shock going from living alone to living with three of them. Boys, I mean. Sometimes I feel like I live in a locker room, after they've been playing basketball or something, and they crowd into this little trailer all sweaty. It's hard to get the air moving.

We stayed at a friend's house the rest of that night, the night of the fire, and camped out on the living room floor. The next morning, we went home and started cleaning up.

Greg opened the door first. I was sort of afraid of what we'd find.

"Hey, check out these windows," Ryan said. He drew a "Z" like Zorro does on the soot covering the living room windows.

The door stuck a little bit. "Some of the panels are warped. I better call the insurance guy," Greg said. Ryan and Daniel followed him inside. I wasn't as curious. I thought about sitting outside all day, but the smoke smell was even stronger next to the black, twisted mess that used to be Jensen's trailer. When I saw that pink-skinned doll on the floor of what used to be their little girl's room, the hair all singed off, I went inside.

Ryan and Daniel were eating Cheerios because they had to catch the bus to school. Greg walked around checking everything out. This was his trailer before I moved in. Everything smelled horrible, but looked okay.

"The phone's not working. I'm going out to get a couple things and call the insurance guy," Greg said. "You boys want a ride to school?"

They nodded with their mouths full, sort of shrugged the way kids do, all boney shoulders and long arms. Ryan wiped his mouth with his sleeve. "I'll get my books."

Ryan and Daniel are good students. They like school. I never really did. Greg was a big athlete at Lincoln High. Football and track mostly. He graduated five years ahead of me, and I didn't grow up here, so I didn't even know who he was.

THE NIGHT AFTER THE FIRE, Greg put up three new fire alarms while I made dinner. The boys watched TV. "The insurance guy said they'd clean the furniture and the carpet. They'd pay to have the curtains cleaned, but we have to take them in someplace ourselves. Just get a receipt. You should call sometime and set up for that service to come. I got the number. I think the phone will be working tomorrow."

I thought about the phone call I made to my mom the day she died. I told her I was pregnant, and she cried because she was happy. I sort of wanted advice but didn't know how to ask for it. I don't know how to ask for anything these days. I just fight down the bile in my throat and try to hide that I'm feeling awful. I flush the toilet a lot in the morning when I'm throwing up. The radio's on kind of loud in the kitchen, and nobody seems to have noticed anything yet. Greg stays up late at night, and he's a pretty heavy sleeper.

I thought about the phone and how I'd never be able to call my mom again. I stood over the stove and fried potatoes and cried. I thought about my big sister, Cora. She was at the funeral too. I hadn't seen her for awhile and she looked different. I mean, I guess we both did. I think your face changes when you're sad. It gets heavy around the eyes.

We both went and visited Dad, but he was still pretty out of it. He said the drugs made him sleepy. He cried and said he didn't mean to leave the windows open at home. He kept talking about the windows in the house and how it might rain in and would we check them? We didn't talk at all about Mom. The doctor said there would be time for that.

So Cora and I went home and slept in our old room before I drove back to Sioux Falls. We stopped the mail and the paper and stacked up all those sympathy cards. Cora got somebody to take care of the house until Dad got better. I watched TV and cried a lot.

Cora rode back with me and flew back to Rapid City from Sioux Falls. I didn't tell her about me being pregnant. It didn't seem like a good time, and I wasn't sure yet if I was going to keep it or not. There was enough to worry about. Besides, Cora and I aren't that close anymore.

Cora kept looking in my eyes, but I don't think she suspected anything, other than how sad I felt about Mom. She told me to call anytime I needed to talk and to come out and visit her. She lives in the Black Hills; she and her boyfriend built a new house. I've never been out to visit her, but I might call her.

"HEY DAD, you going to get your trophies polished up too?" Daniel looked up at his dad who stood on a little step stool putting the screws in a fire alarm over the arch to the hallway. Daniel was talking about Greg's high school trophies that set on the entertainment center above the VCR.

Ryan snickered, but Daniel kept a straight face. "My trophies are fine, smart alack." Greg snapped the batteries in place and put the cover on. He pushed the tester button, and an annoying squeal filled the place.

"Are you sure? I mean, if there's money for restoration, maybe you should get them polished up for free. Can't find trophies like that these days."

Daniel and Ryan don't go out for sports. They're small and skinny like their mother. "Smart little shit," Greg said. "I don't need that from you, okay?"

"What did I say?" Daniel shrugged and held his hands out, palms up.

We sat down to dinner. Everybody was pretty quiet. "You all right?" Greg looked at the small helping on my plate.

"Fine," I said. "Not very hungry, that's all."

I was thinking about babies. Thinking about children

with long arms and big hands. Thinking about fire alarms and photos and broken dolls in the rubble. Something started ringing inside of me like an alarm of my own. Ringing and trembling and making my hands shake as I held the fork. The ringing went on and on through dinner and all that tense talking.

Finally it worked its way to my head, and the pain was awful. I decided to lay down and rest. When Greg came in later, he sat down on the edge of the bed and said he wanted to talk. I thought maybe it was the time I'd tell him I had a baby growing inside of me. Our baby and what should we do? But he was drinking and started talking about high school, and how much more fun life was then, when he got noticed for his talents, and people cheered on Friday nights, and how he didn't understand how his boys could be such smart asses. No respect. And worse yet, no interest in the games he loved to play.

He wondered what he did wrong raising them, but kids were damn hard work, he said, and they never even say thanks. Then he told me good night and went out to watch some cable TV. I heard the announcers call the play by play. College basketball. I heard the buzzer, signaling a substitution, calling for a time out. It went off again and again until I fell asleep.

14

THE ANGLER

The ice cracked deep down below the surface, and it sounded like the moan of a dying animal, a big animal far off somewhere in a cave. Greg tapped the toe of his boot against the crusted snow to keep his foot warm.

"Well, I don't believe it. I mean what kind of a damn queer thing is that to say anyway?" Daryl reeled in his line and checked the bait. He shook his head.

"I've known him for twenty years. Twenty frickin' years. I mean, we were on varsity, for chrissakes."

Greg took a deep breath. The fish house was warm, but there didn't seem to be enough air to breathe. He and Daryl were alone. The other guys had walked up to the cabin about half an hour earlier, after Thomas dropped the bomb and left. To go for a walk, he said. Greg stood, felt the kinks in his back, and walked outside with a beer in his hand. The shadows were long and inky black beside the pine-covered shore. He glanced up the beach looking for a big jacket, a male form, something moving. The ice buckled the night before and left huge, jagged slabs pushed against a small arm of land. It looked like a bulldozer had pushed them there. Broken slabs of concrete. A road they were building over.

The air was cold, and Greg had left his gloves inside the cabin. He felt a pain around his heart and imagined it was an attack of some kind, not the cold air. He was a young man, didn't smoke much, liked a beer or two, but wasn't really the profile for a heart attack victim. Thirty-five years old. Divorced. A father of two. He thought of Caitlyn and her new interest in a child, in marriage, in the whole damn movie all over again. Maybe that was the mysterious pain he was feeling. A small steel trap with jagged teeth trying to grab him by the chest.

HE WALKED BACK into the fish house, rubbing his hands. "This was suppose to be an R&R kind of week. What's going on, anyway?" He looked at Daryl when he asked the question, but it wasn't as if he expected an answer. It was only Wednesday. Four more days with the five of them. Four more days away from the rest of his life. "I wonder why he told us today? Why didn't he wait until later?"

Daryl shrugged. "Hell if I know. What did he think we'd do? Jesus, that's great, now we can go on a date? Weird. Too damn weird for me."

Greg took a shot of schnapps from a pint sitting on the ice between them and reeled in his line. He threw the limp minnow back into the black hole in the ice; it floated belly up in the water.

He'd known these guys since junior high. Every year they made this trip, got drunk, caught fish, played cards, and talked into the night. They talked about wives and girl friends. Jobs. Professional sports. Even the death of Mike's daughter a few years back. They were tight. "Maybe he wanted some time for us to get used to it. Couldn't be that easy to tell us. It's kind of creepy though...when you think about it."

Daryl scratched his red beard and shrugged. "Well, he can find a new bunkmate. I ain't getting naked with a queer in the room." He looked at his watch. "I've had it; they ain't biting. Let's go in."

The two men walked out across the blue ice and snow toward the cabin with the square, yellow windows. A tendril of smoke climbed out of the chimney. Greg could smell the fire before they got off the lake. The burning cedar mixed in with northern Minnesota air. His hopeful eyes scanned the long beach. A downed tree or a big boulder began to look like other things. It was almost dark.

Where would Thomas go? There wasn't another cabin for at least a couple of miles. Greg's stomach turned thinking about the cold—a timber wolf with gray eyes. Stalking, keeping a few steps behind your thoughts. Ready whenever you weren't.

"THROW it on the grass when we drive by." Tom shifted the green Impala and turned onto 12th street. Daryl and Greg sat in the back seat, the naked mannequin pressed between them. Their white T-shirts and canvas sneakers caught the streetlight as they passed. Three boys rode in the front. Short hair. Converse high-tops.

"Coach's light's on. Let's forget it."

"Drive on by."

"Oh, you chickens."

Tom turned off the lights and slowed down. "On three, you guys and don't break her. Get out and lay her on the lawn."

It was ten-thirty at night. The boys found the mannequin sticking out of a dumpster behind Wolfe's department store on main street. Cruising main after a game of three on two.

Greg and Daryl stumbled out of the car, and one of the dummy's feet hit the door as they pulled her out. Toes broke off and landed near the curb. It surprised Greg how fragile the thing was.

Everyone was laughing when they drove away, envisioning her in various compromising positions. The five of them slept in a tent in Greg's yard, and no one else found out about "the gift."

The next day, going in to an early football practice, they drove by the coach's yard. At first glance, Greg thought it looked like one of those lawn ornaments, a deer laying down in the grass, but as they drove by, he could see the bald thing face down on the sod.

"Hey look, she's mooning us," Tom said.

"Coach will probably keep her. Prop her up in the living room for company." Mike took a swig out of a bottle of orange juice.

"I bet he'll keep her in the bedroom," Daryl said. "Coach seems a little off."

The boys piled out of the car and into the locker room for the day's first practice.

"WHO'S FRYING THE FISH?" Wayne tore open a bag of pretzels, poured them in a bowl, and put it on the table. He swung his long leg over the back of the chair and slid back into it. He was six foot four, a good first baseman back in high school with that long reach. Now he worked at 3M in the accounting department.

"I cleaned them." Daryl grabbed a pretzel and studied his cards.

"I'll do it. Who's eating?" Mike looked around the room, scratching his head, fingers lost in thick raven curls. He wondered where Tom was, but didn't say it out loud. Thomas. He wondered where Thomas was. Things change. People grow away. Change their names and walk down the beach without another word. How long had Thomas known? Had he kept it a secret all this time? Wasn't it something you were suppose to be able to tell just by looking at a guy?

Al, Wayne, and Daryl were playing poker. Al's muscle-bound arms perched on the table like two separate animals. "I don't see why he brought it up anyway. Pass." He folded his cards and laid them in a stack in front of him.

Daryl threw three white chips into the anti. "Damn weird if you ask me. I've known him twenty years."

"I wonder if all that time…" Wayne threw in three chips. "Call. I mean, does a guy always know that or does he decide or what?"

Mike stood at the stove and dropped the first walleyes into the hot grease. The fish sizzled and spattered, the smell immediately enough to make everyone realize they were hungry.

"Who cares anyway?" Greg said. "I mean, he's been our friend so long, what difference does it make?" No one answered. The room was quiet except for the wet logs crackling in the fireplace and the sound of frying fish.

Greg looked at the faces of his friends, but he wanted to answer his own question. He wanted to understand what difference this all made. How Thomas must feel. How they would all act from now on when they were together. Any secret kept that long was bound to crack the foundation of a friendship, wasn't it? But how long had Tom known? What was there to "know" anyway?

Greg walked outside onto the front step and shut the door. His breath caught in his throat. It was damn cold. There were stars and a grapefruit moon. It was six-thirty now and dark. Tom had been out there almost three hours. There was no place to go, and the temperature was dropping.

Greg shook his head and ran his fingers through his hair. He was graying at the temples, getting older. He thought about Caitlyn and his boys back in Sioux Falls. He wondered how cold it was and if they'd gotten any snow. Caitlyn was good with the boys. So patient. Better than their own mother had been. Better than he was. It didn't make sense that he and Caitlyn fought so much these days, but she kept pushing him, always trying to change him into someone else.

Greg took a deep breath and screamed "Tom!...Thomas!" The sound was pulled from his mouth out into the intense cold. Before it had dissolved completely, all the men were on the porch in their stocking feet and flannel shirts screaming, a jumble of cries:

"Thomas!"

"Hey, Tom!"

"Dinner, man. Thomas! Come on in. It's time to eat."

"Hey, Tommy, where are you man?"

Greg got the keys to the snowmobile, grabbed a hat, some extra gloves, and a down sleeping bag and came back out on the porch. The others were still standing there, their hands in their pockets, frosted air coming out of their mouths like steam. "I'm going to go have a look around. If he gets back blink the porch light for awhile, would you?"

"Sure. You want me to come along?" Mike asked.

"No. If I find him, he can ride back with me."

The "if" of that comment sat heavy in the air.

"He can't be far away," Wayne said.

"Nah, he's fine." Daryl's voice was subdued and hesitant.

The men filed back inside when Greg started the snowmobile and headed down to the shore.

BACK IN HIGH SCHOOL, Greg and Tom were probably the closest. Greg thought about the time they painted the art teacher's house as a summer job. An old three-story Victorian up on the hill near the prison. It took all summer to scrape and paint that thing. They made a little money, but mostly they had time to talk and screw around. Miss Magney was young and single, and both boys were intrigued to be around her house, working near the windows, looking in on her private life. She listened to classical music all day and sculpted in a studio in her attic. All of her art was made from stuff you find in nature: bones, feathers, driftwood. Sort of primitive and spooky, the boys thought then.

There was a rumor that she fell in love with a man who was sent to the prison, and she moved into that house to be near him. Rumors were always raging about the young teachers.

Greg thought about that summer. Had he and Tom ever talked about girls? Surely they must have. None of the guys dated much in high school. There was always too much to do. Football, basketball, baseball, or track. Always some practice. Always some game. They were a close group of boys who liked a quick game of two on two, a weekend fishing at the lake, a bike race to the Pizza Shack across town. They thrived on athletic competition so much that they were almost seniors before they discovered girls. Then Greg was married and divorced before many of his classmates had finished college.

Tom was a joker. Always daring others to do some crazy thing. The leader. The get-away car. He was never the one taking the risk, except the time he climbed the water tower and wrote "Let It Be" with purple spray paint.

GREG SCANNED THE SHORE. It was snowing lightly. He rode about a mile-and-a-half from the cabin, then the shore curved to the north. He followed some tracks but was losing them and needed to decide if he should follow the shore or turn inland.

He turned off the motor and sat for a moment to think when he saw the footprints again, up the beach, leading into a small moonlit clearing.

"Tom? Thomas?" His voice was soft, hesitant in the shadowed, dark envelope of night. He stood up and tried again. "Thomas!" This time it echoed. There was a long pause and then a reply.

"Over here."

Greg turned and saw his friend fifty feet away, sitting in the bottom branch of an old pine, his feet tucked up under him. "God." Greg sighed with relief and sat back down on the seat of his snowmobile. Finally, he got up and walked over toward the tree. "You scared the shit out of us, you know. What are you doing here? You okay?"

"Fine. A little cold."

"A little dense. You want to freeze?" Greg felt comfortable now, seeing his friend, slipping into the old roles. "Get out of that tree, would you? You planning on spending the night or what?"

Tom shrugged. "I thought maybe I'd bag a wolf and then ride it back. I've been hearing a few howl."

"Yeah, and they're talking smorgasbord on a Scandinavian white boy." Greg shook his head and smiled. The moon made it easy to see. Thomas slipped out of the tree, stretched his arms and legs. "You think I'd come out looking for you?"

"Not really, why?"

"What were you going to do?"

"I was sitting and thinking, man. Do I have to report to you or what?"

"No." Greg looked at the ground, then at Tom's thin gloves. "I got some choppers along. Want them?"

"I'd give you a crisp fifty for them about now."

"You could have come back you know."

"Yeah, I know, but the birds ate all the bread crumbs I'd trailed. Couldn't find my way." Thomas paused a minute. "What are they saying back there?"

"Not much."

"Liar."

"Okay. There's a little talk. Some confusion. Some surprise."

"And a hell of a lot of discomfort," Thomas said.

"I don't know. Mostly everyone was worried about you out here."

"Right. That's exactly the reaction I saw on all the shocked faces when I told you."

"What did you expect? We didn't know. We were surprised. Is that so awful?"

Thomas didn't answer. He shoved the thick gloves over his thin pair and pushed his hands into the pockets of his parka.

"I left all of them standing out on the porch in their stocking feet screaming their heads off calling you. Telling you to get your ass inside. Telling you to come back."

"And what are you thinking?" Thomas looked right at Greg.

"I've been thinking about painting Magney's house the summer after our junior year. How we sat up on that scaffold and talked for hours. About the time we dumped the mannequin on coach's lawn. About the times we rode our bikes out to the pit to go swimming." Greg stopped. "I've been thinking about my friend. Wondering what all this means. How long you've known you were gay. I mean, is it something you decide or something you just find out? I been wondering if you're happy. If this is going to change all of us. How I'm suppose to act."

"I don't know." Thomas' voice was softer now. His brow was wrinkled. Frost covered the fox fur around the hood of his coat. "I only know I couldn't keep it a secret anymore, even if I lost all of you for friends. My life's almost half over. I just want to be myself."

"I've never known anybody who's gay."

"You've known somebody who's gay for over twenty years, Greg."

"Yeah, I guess I have." Greg smiled.

"You don't have to worry. You're my friend. You've always been a friend. That's all I'm interested in."

"I don't know about the guys. I think…"

"You don't have to think for them. I'll talk to everybody myself. I just wanted a give you all a few hours to think about it. But I tell you what, I'm cold. You going to give me a ride back on that snowmobile or what?"

"There's fresh walleye for dinner," Greg said. "I caught them all myself."

"Yeah, right. And ten bucks says I catch the most tomorrow."

"You got a bet." Greg started the engine. The light of the snowmobile penetrated the tree-lined shore. The pines and birch stood tall and crowded together. A sort of shelter. A fortress from the cold.

15

AISLE 5

I was working the four to twelve, getting carts in from the parking lot when I first saw her. It was cold, sort of snowing, and I didn't pay much attention at first. I thought maybe she forgot where her car was parked, walking around like that.

Vern, that's the manager, kicked butt if we didn't hurry when we got the carts, and I'd forgotten my gloves anyway; it was freezing. Friday nights were the worst. Everybody in town was buying groceries and stocking up for their parties; it was New Year's Eve. Anyway, I saw her out in the lot. She was holding her coat shut around her. She was real tall, that's what I noticed first, and she had this long red hair that was blowing around in the wind and snow. I went inside.

I was stocking aisle five when I saw her again. Five is the diaper aisle, and she stood down at the end near the stacks of pink Pampers. She was wearing black stretch pants; I guess I noticed her long legs. I don't know how old she was, and it's not like I was going to hit on her; I was just taking a look. She was standing there and the next thing I know she's crying. Kind of quiet like and not making a big show, but she was crying all right. I opened a carton of newborns and tried to mind my own business. I was starting to feel sort of weird about it, like I felt sorry for her or something.

Lately, when people cry, it makes me feel like I'm in a hospital, and there are monitors everywhere and all that beeping. Blue screens, yellow lines. Green screens, white lines. Red blinking lights. Beep. Pause. Beep. Who would have ever thought a seventeen-year-old guy would spend a whole summer sitting in a hospital room watching his best friend's body fight back? Now Kyle has a new heart, and we drive out to the mall on Friday nights, and I'm back at work. He wants to play catch and go biking, but I don't trust his heart as much as he does. I always talk him into a movie. Say I'm tired from working or something.

So I emptied two more cartons, and she was still standing there. "Can I help you?" I finally asked. My chest felt tight, and I was kind of uneasy.

She jumped, like she was a little startled. Maybe embarrassed. "No, but thanks."

Then we both just stood there. I didn't know how to leave, and she didn't seem to want to, so I looked at the floor and then straightened a couple of rows of pull-ups. "You got a kid?" I asked. I don't know why I said that. She didn't want any help, but I looked right at her. She kind of smiled.

"Sort of," she said. "I'm pregnant."

"Hey, great." I smiled and felt my face get red. Pregnant women embarrass me. It's like I can see through their clothes or something, like I've just heard about the details of their female anatomy. Kind of like saying the word "breast"... it doesn't feel natural. I shrugged and thought about walking away.

"Yeah. I suppose." She smiled a little again and brushed the hair from her face. Long red hair. She was real pretty.

"Well, if there's anything I can do...." I was so damn stupid. I sounded like...I don't know what. I remembered that she'd said earlier she didn't need any help. I shrugged and headed down to the other end of the aisle, pulled a couple boxes of baby shampoo off the cart, and started shelving again.

When Kyle first found out he needed a new heart, we were juniors and had just started football practice in the fall. It took ten months to get a heart, I mean to find a donor. Some guy on a motorcycle got hit by a car, and Kyle was on the table hours later getting his heart. It seemed really gross at first. I guess I hadn't thought much about life and death and all that. And then I spent almost a whole summer in the Sioux River Hospital sitting in a maroon chair near a steel bed, surrounded by machines. Kyle's father's dead and his mother works, so I stayed there. He's my best friend. I read the sports page to him every day and *Sports Illustrated* cover to cover. We watched game shows and talked about friends from school. We didn't talk about the guy on the motorcycle until this Christmas. Even then, when I saw him cry for the first time, I worried it was too hard on his heart. I know I shouldn't worry, they say he's just fine, but I can't help it.

"You okay?" She was standing next to me. I guess I was standing there like a dolt, looking at the shelves. My face felt hot. I shook my head. "Yeah. God, it's been a long day."

"I'm Caitlyn. Happy New Year." She held out her hand.

I shook it; I didn't know what else to do. "I'm Tim."

"Not a great night to be working, huh?" She smiled again.

"It's not so bad," I didn't mention the time-and-a-half. I didn't figure it was cool to talk to a customer about money. She stood there a while, and I couldn't think of a thing to say. I just wanted her to leave. I felt uncomfortable and couldn't figure out why she was there. She didn't even look pregnant. Then I got this idea that maybe she was shoplifting, like with a partner, and she was suppose to keep me busy. "Excuse me," I said and did a quick aisle check. I didn't expect to see anyone; it was almost twelve and the place had emptied out except for a few stragglers picking up more seltzer and soda for their parties. At least I expected her to be gone when I got back.

I had two boxes left to empty, then I could clean up and go home. I just wanted to leave. Luckily, when I got back to aisle five she wasn't there. I tore down the boxes and went in back for my coat. After I punched out, I walked past the registers to leave, and she was standing in lane three. She paid for a box of newborn diapers and was holding the bag close to her chest. I walked out first and didn't really look at her.

I was scraping off the windows of my truck when she walked by. "Have a nice night," she said. Like she knew me. Like she was my mother or sister or something. I didn't answer her. I didn't know her, and I didn't want to talk anymore. She walked out of the lot and turned up Willow towards the pricey housing development.

All the way home, I thought about her long legs and that baby growing inside of her. Two hearts beating in one body. It was snowing pretty hard and the wipers were batting away the snow. I stuck in a tape and sang to myself, but I couldn't forget how it felt to see her cry.

I kept making up stories, giving her a story of her own. She was rich, and her husband didn't want the kid.

She was poor, and she didn't want the kid. She was rich, and the father was poor. She was sick and shouldn't have a kid. The kid was sick and shouldn't be born. The woman wasn't pregnant at all; she was a scam artist, shoplifting food. She was pregnant, and she needed a friend. She was twenty and looked older. She was thirty and looked twenty-two. She thought I was handsome. She thought something was wrong with me— standing like a zombie staring at baby shampoo. Wondering if my best friend was going to have too much fun this New Year's Eve and make his heart work so hard that it stalled out on him. Wondering if the biker who had the heart first was a strong guy. Wondering what a strong guy was. Wondering how strong a heart really was. Wondering how much was muscle and how much was something else.

16

SPYING

I t's not like I sit in the porch all day and stare out the window at them or anything. I mean, I'm not that kind of person. My Aunt Elaine made a hobby of that in Albert Lea, always looking across the courtyard at the Garrison's place, trying to see if any bikers in leather jackets were visiting. She seemed to think they belonged to some group, like a devil cult or something, just because some of their friends drove Harleys. How stupid.

I just noticed one weekend, after Jill left for work, that Roger got right in his car and brought back this other woman. They sat out in their screened-in porch and drank Budweiser from the can. When she first started hanging around, I thought she was a relative, like a sister or some-thing. I don't know them that well, and I never would've asked. Anyway, this blonde showed up, and they sat out there in the porch drinking and talking for hours. I didn't see them touch once, but I decided they were just trying to put on a good show for the neighbors, in case anybody got snoopy and let Jill in on all this.

Jill's a nurse and works graveyard sometimes, so I suppose Roger thought it was pretty easy to get by with the whole thing. I remember seeing the blonde prancing around in her dark sunglasses when Jill still worked at Northwestern. Now she's down at County General, so it's been going on a long time. It was even before Percy, my boyfriend, got the job selling shoes at Daytons, and it seems like he's been there forever.

Anyway, I don't spy on them or anything, but I think it's pretty disgusting that Roger carries on like that right in front of the whole world. Jill's probably the only one that doesn't know, and I'm not going to tell her. I mean, it's none of my business.

I gave up that sort of thing when I told my best friend Carrie Louise what her husband said to me at the last New Year's Eve party. She hasn't talked to me much since, like it was my idea or something. Some people just don't play with a full deck. I wouldn't have jumped in the sack with her fat old husband if he was the last guy on the planet, and she should've known it.

But anyway, I was sitting in the porch this afternoon thinking about things, and those two happened to be out on the lawn stripping paint off of an old rocking chair, like this woman lived there or something, and they were refinishing some furniture for their own house. It burned me up knowing Jill was working and probably thinking things were going along just fine, and he was out there snapping old rags at the blonde's rump and flirting to beat all hell... right out in the open.

The chair was kind of a cantaloupe color, and after a couple of hours I could start to see the oak grain coming through. The back was pretty solid, two main pieces with an oval hole in the middle. Not all those spindles. That's the hardest part, getting all the paint out of those little cracks.

I used to refinish a lot of furniture myself. My house is full of antiques. Percy helped sometimes. These days he plays racquetball and runs circles around the lake. When he became a salesman and started wearing a tie to work, he seemed to get a different idea about himself. He buys fancy clothes now and only likes those old movies in black and white. He said regular TV was "shallow" and then went out and bought a VCR when we really needed a dehumidifier for the basement. So now he watches Hepburn and Tracy movies night after night.

YEAH, I work. But there are bills and some money has to go in those envelopes, doesn't it? I mean, I'm not complaining. I pay the utilities and keep my mouth shut.

I answer phones part-time down at a mortgage company on fifth. It pays okay, and I might get into some other job there. A promotion, I mean. They seem to like me. Once in awhile I meet Percy for lunch, but lately he's been spending more time at the health club showing off. Shoes for running. Shoes for racquetball. Gloves for this. A Gore-Tex suit for that. The club is seventy-five bucks a month. Well, I guess it's his money.

I used to like our neighbor Roger okay, but these days he comes out of the house smiling and shouting hello like nothing at all is wrong, and I want to just shove him under my car and drive away.

I always told Mom that if Dad really did leave her, after all that talk, I'd personally help her hunt him down and string him up by his feet from some tree until he apologized and promised to come back home to us. But then his heart got him before Elinor Huntsbury did, whatever that's worth.

Percy's family is so perfect; he can't understand what I worry about.

He says I have to trust him. I hear that over and over again, but sometimes I just wonder who he finds so interesting down at that club. We used to spend our time together, and now he just can't wait to get out of the house at night and run in circles until he sweats. Even in the winter with a foot or two of snow on the ground, he goes out there looking like a model for some L.L. Bean catalogue, down to the forty dollar jogging shoes. And I sit in the pressed-back rocker by the fireplace and watch logs disappear.

Yesterday, when Jill was home working in the marigolds, I decided to go out and see how she was, you know, if she wanted to talk or anything. I took my paper and my lawn chair out the front door, ready to glance up and look surprised that she was out there, but she dusted off her knees and disappeared in the front door before I even got the chair unfolded. Seemed like a sure sign to me that Jill knew more that I thought. God, the poor thing probably didn't feel like talking about it.

I don't think I'd ever leave Percy. He thinks I need him, and maybe he's right, but I'm not even sure of that anymore. It's almost fall, and all I've got to look forward to is a bunch of dry leaves taking a dive from the trees and ending up in a black plastic bag by the street. Maybe I need a hobby, but it all seems like too much work. I like the warm sun in the porch windows. I like the way the shadows look on the wall. Some days I just sit out in the hammock and think about being little again, following the fence down to the field where all the daisies bloomed. The same path the cows took at night when they came to the barn, each one walking slow, looking straight ahead.

Maybe I will go back to work. Maybe I'll call and tell them I'm sorry, tell them I'd like to give it another try. I'm not really working there right now. We had sort of a misunderstanding, but I'm sure I won't have any trouble getting my job back. It might be nice to get out of the house again.

Percy's working the Twelve Hour Sale tonight. I still haven't finished caning the seat of the old oak rocker upstairs. If I get it done, I might give it to Mom for her birthday. She's getting older. A person should have a nice chair to sit in by the fire.

17

THE DANCER

Sitting on a bar stool, waiting to order a cup of coffee, he watched the young people walking in. It was eight-fifteen. The band didn't start playing until nine o'clock.

The back wall of the bar was mirrored. It made Arthur uncomfortable to look at himself, made him feel conspicuous. He noticed a framed picture of a Great Dane in a showman's stance near the cash register.

"May I help you?"

"Yes. I'm sorry. I'd like a cup of coffee, please. With cream."

"Coming up," the young woman replied, turning to the coffee maker behind her. She wore jeans and a striped shirt with a bow tie. "You like my dog?"

"Pardon me?"

"My dog," she said, tilting her head toward the picture.

"Oh. Yes. It's a fine animal. Do you show him?"

"Yeah, I show him off in here and around the lakes every afternoon, but that's about it." The bartender smiled. "We used to do shows when I was younger. But now I just use all that training to keep Jack in line whenever we're in a crowd."

"Jack?"

"Yeah, Jack Daniels," she smiled. "This bar had no influence on the name though. I picked it out long before I worked here. Reminded me of a pirate's name. I think Jack would like sailing the seven seas."

She helped another customer at the end of the bar. Arthur turned again, looking over the crowd. It was the first time he'd been to the Kite House. Maybe tonight he would dance. Leaning over the counter, resting his elbows, he slowly stirred his coffee.

"A pound of hamburger a day," the woman said, wiping off the bar in front of Arthur.

"Pardon me?"

"A pound of hamburger. That's what that dog eats every day, along with his dry dog food. I have to keep my refrigerator full of that stuff, and I don't eat meat at all. Kind of funny, huh?"

"Yes." Creases formed around Arthur's eyes when he

smiled. His face was framed with white hair that ran like a hedge around the brown dome of his head. The woman's energy delighted him.

"You have one?" she asked.

"Two. Dobermans. Lovely dogs, really. Lovely."

"My name's Holly." She reached her hand across the bar. "Nice to meet you."

"Arthur." He shook her hand firmly. "The pleasure is mine. Entirely."

"I bet you get as much grief about Dobermans as I get about a Dane. People frighten so easily, you know? Are yours guard dogs? I mean, are they friendly or all business?"

"Friendly. Completely harmless. I'm not sure a burglar would agree with me," Arthur said. "I don't think they'd be too friendly if someone tried crawling in my kitchen window, but they are quite the comedians, really. Wonderful companions."

"What do you do, Arthur?" Holly washed glasses as she talked, looking over her work directly at him.

"I'm retired."

"No kidding! How old are you? You don't look that old. I mean, well, you know." Holly shrugged her right shoulder.

"Sixty-seven. And thank you."

He figured Holly was in her late twenties. It interested

him that retired sounded ancient, older than he could possibly be. People were starting to crowd near the bar; waitresses began placing an occasional order. He thought about leaving the house tonight. Had he left out water for the dogs? He remembered locking the backdoor again after walking them, but had he left their water out? After their long run today, they would need water; he tried to remember. It frustrated him that the details weren't clear; so many things happened by habit that it was too easy to forget about them altogether. He couldn't remember and tried to think about something else.

He thought about training dogs, the trainer-animal relationship. During the war he had worked with surveillance dogs that guarded the military compound. It seemed more like a hobby, befriending dogs that scared everyone except the hand that fed them, the hand that stroked their fur when they obeyed precisely. They'd used shepherds then, but Dobermans were more to Arthur's liking. He admired the beautiful dogs, their speed and strength coupled with their grace and fine definition. People often misunderstood dogs, like Holly said. They weren't always what they seemed.

When Holly walked by, she tipped her head over his empty coffee cup.

"Another?" she asked, backing away as she moved down the bar.

"No, thank you. I believe I'll have a scotch and water."

"Pardon?" Holly was at the other end of the bar now, eyebrows raised.

"Scotch and water," he said, raising his voice slightly.

"Coming up."

THE FIVE-PIECE ROCK band started their first number as Arthur felt the initial hints of alcohol in his stomach. The large room was filling quickly, absorbing the music. Colored lights soaked into his pale shirt. Looking around, he noticed the clothes the kids were wearing: white cotton shirts, thin ties, black shoes. Clothes like those hanging in the back of his closet, now the latest style. The clothes were new to them. Kids needed change as much as anyone, needed new things to hold on to. This could be any bar thirty or forty years ago, he thought. I could have been one of those kids.

A couple, about nineteen or twenty, moved out onto the dance floor when the tempo of the music picked up. Arthur stood up and leaned on the bar, watching, remembering when he would have been the first one out there, swinging Lucille about like an extension of his own arm. They were quite the dancers. People used to buy them drinks if they would go out and dance again. Saturday nights were filled with laughter and exercise, the joy of being a part of the music. He had always enjoyed dancing.

Three young men sat at a nearby table covered with empty beer pitchers. They looked like college boys; one was wearing a letter jacket, another a torn football jersey. The third, in a flannel shirt and paint-stained jeans, poured beer, refilling their glasses.

"Hey, old man, you looking for your daughter or something?" The guy in the letter jacket yelled just as the band finished a song. They all leaned back in their chairs, laughing.

Arthur turned and replied, "Good evening." Politely and smoothly, he carried the phrase like the host of some great musical event. Then turning, he canvassed the bar for a dance partner. It was time; tonight he would dance.

The huge room was crowded with tables. Nearly every one was filled with young people pouring from iced pitchers of beer, smoking or chewing gum, eyes always moving. Arthur was amazed at the amount of movement even off the dance floor. Each time he caught a woman's eyes, she averted them. Looking around the room, he felt like he was prying, being too personal. He got up and walked to a table near the bar where two women were sitting alone. He asked the first one that looked at him, "Excuse me, do you care to dance?"

"No. I'm busy, thanks," she answered, staring out over her glass.

Arthur thought it only polite to ask her companion. He swallowed hard. "Excuse me, would you care to dance?" The second woman ignored him completely, as if he would go away if she pretended he wasn't there. She reaching into her purse and pulled out a cigarette.

Arthur bowed slightly and moved away. As he turned back toward the bar, a young woman waving off to his left caught his eye. She smiled and motioned for him to come over.

"You looking for a dance partner?" she asked, her voice energetic and friendly. Her long blonde hair was pulled off the sides of her face with clips. She leaned forward on the table, her fingernails tapping time to the music.

"Yes, I am. Would you care to?" Arthur asked.

"Sure, let's go!"

She stood up and took his hand, leading him to the dance floor. Arthur was caught off guard and followed her toward the band, weaving through the crowd. He was surprised at her bold act of reaching for his hand, but hers was warm and relaxed. He longed to make his own cold fingers feel the same.

Once on the dance floor, he suddenly felt the rock-and-roll music was completely foreign. Feeling awkward and icy stiff, he watched his partner's movements, imitating them as closely as possible. "Good," she shouted. "Hey, anything goes; you're doing fine! Just move around any way you want to!"

Arthur slid his feet along the floor, remembering the days when the sand made a soft grating sound beneath his shoes, remembering the measured steps and turns. He smiled and swayed even more with the strong bass beat. Once more comfortable, he took her hands and began incorporating a few of the old steps with the new music. She was a good dancer and picked up quickly. As he warmed up, the music's tempo pulsed in his ears; his tight shoulders relaxed. Every step became an important part of the song. Arthur clapped as the music ended.

His partner smiled, holding out her hand. "Thanks. My name is Rita. That was fun," she said, winded. "You do really well. You're hardly out of breath!"

Arthur wanted to return her thanks, but his shyness returned. He nodded his head, smiled and turned to walk back to the bar. Holly was busier now, the bar was nearly full. Waitresses stood in line with orders, crowding near the till. While waiting to order another drink, Arthur thought about the dogs again. It was still warm enough in the evening that they would be uncomfortable if they were thirsty and he had forgotten to put water out before he left.

That afternoon they walked further than usual, the autumn sun warm and refreshing. Arthur took the two Dobermans along the river all the way up to the old mill.

Holiday and Whitman enjoyed snooping around the railroad tracks, running up and down the banks, scaring up squirrels and birds, chasing an occasional butterfly. They walked a couple of miles, and the interstate highway noises were replaced by birds filling the tall trees that hugged the houses along the river. Arthur chose to rest on a pile of old railroad ties while the dogs showed off for him, retrieving plastic bags and scraps of paper. He let the sun soak into his brown corduroy trousers and plaid lumberman's jacket, warming him and his tired muscles.

"You two aren't a bit tired are you?" he asked as the two sleek dogs sat down, side by side, in front of him, ears alert, ready to fetch. "Holiday, stay. Whitman, down." The dogs obeyed his command as he reached into his pocket for the bag of apple slices. He placed one on his left shoe and one on his right, as the dogs remained still as death. "Holiday, okay!" he said. The dog jumped up, ran to his left shoe and ate the piece of fruit in one quick gulp. Licking her chops, looking at the right shoe and then at Whitman, she whined softly in her throat. "No, girl. Now Holiday, down. Whitman, okay!"

It was their game. Curiously enough, both dogs liked apples and eagerly awaited the afternoon treat. Holiday only went to the left shoe, Whitman to the right. After the apples, they always started home.

Holly walked up. "Another, Arthur?"

"Yes, thank you." One more. It was early, he would

not be able to sleep, and the bar was not so crowded that he felt pushed out, not yet. The Kite House was close; he could walk home in a few minutes. Arthur lived in the same house for seventeen years, but he had never been in the bar.

More frequently since July, however, he was having trouble sleeping. Even though he took the dogs on long walks and tended his yard and garden, he didn't seem to tire. Instead, he grew restless and thought about long ago, the soft shoe, the big bands, and Lucille. He spent evenings rearranging the small house, watching late movies, and reading the paper a second time.

REACHING FOR HIS DRINK, Arthur's arm was jostled by a woman standing very close to him, so near he could smell her perfume. Three guys from the table nearby stood behind her holding their beer mugs in their hands. The freckled one in the red flannel shirt spoke. "Hey, mister, we think we found your daughter. She's sorry for hanging out in this nasty old bar and will go home with you now, right honey?"

The other two men laughed. The young woman shrugged her shoulders, smiling. "Wanna boogie?" she asked, half under her breath.

Arthur took a deep breath, hesitating, looking at his shoes.

"Didn't you hear the nice lady? If she ain't your daughter and you don't wanna dance with her, why are you here, man?"

Arthur decided not to acknowledge the men. He turned to the woman at his side. "Excuse me, I thought it would be all right." He looked straight into her eyes. "I thought I was old enough to do what I wanted. I just like to dance."

The woman took a few steps back, the teasing smile gone from her face. Arthur excused himself, nodded to Holly as she walked up and said, "Good night. Take care of that Jack Daniels. And thanks for the conversation."

"Hey, you too." Holly glanced from his full glass to the three men around him. "And come again soon. Really."

Arthur made his way through the crowded room toward the door. He passed Rita's table where she sat talking to a couple of men, laughing, brushing her fine hair off her shoulders. She looked up as he stopped.

"Thank you for the lovely dance. Good night."

"Anytime." She smiled. "And thank you."

Outside the air was cool and fresh compared to the smoke-filled bar. Arthur adjusted his jacket, buttoning it, smoothing his hair with his hand. On the corner of Hamilton and 60th, he bent over toward the dispenser to read the headlines in the city paper. Still Saturday's edition; he'd read that one. Perhaps the gas station on

62nd would have an early Sunday edition. He wasn't tired and felt like working a good crossword puzzle or maybe reading the funnies.

The dogs did need water. He remembered washing out their bowls before he left the house. He hadn't refilled them, now he was sure of it. Picking up his step, he hurried home in the late night quiet.

Remembering

Is what you do. Stand at the back door
Looking over the yard in the early morning,
Count grapefruit trees, count birds on the wire,
Count each breath—in
And then out.
Count the times you can remember
Every word he said with love, every
Smile across the room at the end of the day
As he glanced in the mirror, switched off
The lights, ran his hand across the counter
One more time.
Remembering is what you do.
You remember because it fills your lungs
And helps you get to the next breath. Remember
Because it fills your heart and coaxes it
To keep on beating. Remember
Because love makes us strong enough
To remember, and remembering might be
The edge of bliss, might be
all that we have until.

ACKNOWLEDGMENTS

"Fire" appeared in *The Lake Street Review*, Vol.15

"The End of Summer" appeared in *Sing Heavenly Muse!*, Vol.9

"Letters Home" appeared in *Mpls. St. Paul Magazine*

"The Dancer" appeared in *The Lake Street Review*, Vol.21

ABOUT THE AUTHOR

Kathleen Patrick is a poet and fiction writer who grew up on the prairies of the Midwest, riding horses, jumping rope, hula hooping, and writing poetry. Her bestselling book, *Airmail: A Story of War in Poems*, centers on her family's experience with wars, from the Vietnam War to the present. *Mercy*, her first novel, is a coming-of-age story set in 1970 on the plains of South Dakota. *Anxiety in the Wilderness* is her first collection of short stories. *Perfume River,* a novel for adults, is a story about anxiety and hope, about believing in the future and reconciling the past.

ALSO BY KATHLEEN PATRICK

Airmail: A Story of War in Poems

"I read it in one sitting and thoroughly enjoyed (if that's the right word) every poem." —Tim O'Brien, author of *The Things They Carried*

"Airmail: A Story of War in Poems…is a great example of how letters and conversations can be turned into stunning poetry. Patrick shares the words and thoughts of seven uncles who served in the military, five of them in Southeast Asia during the American war in Vietnam. …It's always cool to see letters sent home from war turned into poems. They become letters from America sent back to America. Kathleen Patrick shows us what it can look like when it's done poetically and done right." —Bill McCloud, The VVA Veteran magazine

"Love the voice and reading pace. It's great and the content is amazing. I am a Vietnam vet and I can relate 100%. Thanks for taking the time to do this project." —J.I.

"Some very strong work here, grounded in correspondence that Kathleen had with her uncles while they served in Vietnam, and also in their correspondence with their parents, subsequent interviews, etc. An amazing piece of work. This is the best war lit I have read since *The Things they Carried* by Tim O'Brien." —P.L.

"A story that stays with you. I read a lot of historical fiction surrounding WWI and II, but this collection of poems highlighting the perspectives of a family living through Vietnam was just as beautiful. Reading poetry framed as letters by young men wanting to serve and the loved ones they left behind was powerfully written and even more powerful in the things that were left unsaid. This is a collection that should be read slowly, absorbing the words from each letter. —A. C.

"Wow…Honestly, I don't read a lot of poetry and didn't think I would like it. However, I loved it; it sucked me right in, and I thought it was beautifully done." —L.M.

"This collection distills so much family history into consumable little poems that will leave you wrecked in the best possible way. A beautiful read." —H.C.

"*Airmail: A Story of War in Poems* is a book about going off to war, a book about coming back home, and a book about those who are left behind." —Kathleen Patrick

Mercy

"*Mercy* is a phenomenal young adult coming of age story that will capture the hearts of readers of all ages!"—K.C.

"*Mercy* is a story of adolescence, but adults would love it as well. It explores the emotional turbulence inherent in dysfunctional families and what it takes to move from dysfunction to love to mercy. Any book that can make me cry and laugh out loud is a winner. *Mercy* is a winner!"—J.C.

"A coming of age, found family, young adult novel. A heartwarming story about a twelve-year-old girl named Sadie who finds the family she always craved in her uncle on a farm. After Sadie's mother struggles with gambling addiction after her father's departure, Sadie has a life of instability and worry. Great short read. The only thing I have to say bad about the story is that it simply isn't long enough!"—K.F.

"Mercy was just a great story and a breath of fresh air!" —L.P.

"Mercy is a story about compassion and kindness. It celebrates the idea families can come in all shapes and sizes and consists of people who support one another, even when it isn't easy. It is a story that reverberates with the basic human need to be loved."—Kathleen Patrick

Anxiety in the Wilderness

"A book of short stories that can only be described as bittersweet. Some parts defiantly pulled at my heartstrings. The author herself said the book was written over a long time period. This comes across in the different scenarios in which the characters are involved in. Each a little exceptional tale of it's own. I especially liked the crossover of characters. I am now patiently waiting for a full novel set in the Iowa wilderness!" —K. F., Goodreads review

"The poetic language of the stories lends a warmth to the storytelling that helps to bring the characters to life. Each story describes a different human worry or anxiety that we all may have experienced at some point in our lives; therefore, each story is relatable in its own way.…Short stories are a disappearing art form, and Patrick demonstrates why we should keep them around. There is no grandiosity of language that detracts from the storyline or from the artful character descriptions. Characters navigate their way through their predicaments one day at a time. The poignant vignettes showcase the rawness of various human emotions, much like a snapshot of an expert photographer. " —B. M., Goodreads Review

"I loved this book! From beginning to end the characters smack of realism and you can see people you know or yourself in them. I wish it were the first book I a series of ten — because I wanted more!"

Perfume River

"The characters are well drawn, and the story is both touching and humorous. Worth the read!" E.S.

"Patrick's prose is smooth, even, and consistent. As with her other work, her use of words is sparse and succinct leaving the reader to indulge in their own imaginings of the space and events. The pauses and silences are evocative." J.S.

"Absolutely loved the main character! Great read!" K. K.

"I enjoy Kathleen Patrick's concise descriptive abilities sprinkled with emotional and intellectual truths." CT

"It is a beautifully written novel with deep feelings. It is the kind of book that wins prizes." E.S.

PLEASE REVIEW THIS BOOK!

Reviews help authors more than you might think. Sometimes they even help readers decide what to read. If you liked *Anxiety in the Wilderness,* please consider writing a review on Amazon and your social media platforms. It can be a few words or a few short sentences. I would greatly appreciate it.

FREE STORY

Sign up for my mailing list at the address below and get a free short story! "Anxiety in the Wilderness" is the title story from my recent collection of short stories by the same title.

https://patrickpoetry.com/

www.ingramcontent.com/pod-product-compliance
Lightning Source LLC
Chambersburg PA
CBHW050847180626
46814CB00007B/2667